"If a woman makes love with a man, it's because she wants to . . . even if she won't admit it to herself," Abby said.

"That's an interesting hypothesis," Joe said softly. "We could . . ." he ran a single finger up the line of her calf to her bare thigh, "put it to the test."

"Oh, Lord," she whispered in comic, but very real, alarm. "You've turned it on full force now, haven't you?" She wrapped her arms around her waist as a shiver of awareness shook her body.

"Don't you realize that practically everything you've said tonight has made me even more intrigued than I was before?" His husky chuckle sent shivers in her running in all directions.

"Don't be intrigued," she said helplessly. "Whatever I said, I take it all back."

"Too late. You see, you said you didn't see anything between us to get so intense about—which makes me very much want to show you just how much there really is to get intense about."

Abby gave a startled laugh, then said, "I think it's at this point I'm supposed to play the outraged female and say something silly like 'How dare you' or 'Of all the nerve'."

"Yes," he agreed softly, examining her face with sharp eyes that were filled with speculation. "And I wonder why you

You're not the only

WHAT ARE *LOVESWEPT* ROMANCES?

They are stories of true romance and touching emotion. We believe those two very important ingredients are constants in our highly sensual and very believable stories in the LOVESWEPT line. Our goal is to give you, the reader, stories of consistently high quality that may sometimes make you laugh, sometimes make you cry, but are always fresh and creative and contain many delightful surprises within their pages.

Most romance fans read an enormous number of books. Those they truly love, they keep. Others may be traded with friends and soon forgotten. We hope that each *LOVESWEPT* romance will be a treasure—a "keeper." We will always try to publish

LOVE STORIES YOU'LL NEVER FORGET
BY AUTHORS YOU'LL ALWAYS REMEMBER

The Editors

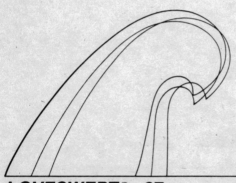

LOVESWEPT® • 87

Billie Green
Dreams of Joe

BANTAM BOOKS
TORONTO • NEW YORK • LONDON • SYDNEY • AUCKLAND

DREAMS OF JOE

A Bantam Book / April 1985

ISBN 0-553-21661-9

Published simultaneously in the United States and Canada

---

*Bantam Books are published by Bantam Books, Inc. Its
trademark, consisting of the words "Bantam Books" and
the portrayal of a rooster, is Registered in U.S. Patent and
Trademark Office and in other countries. Marca Registrada.
Bantam Books, Inc., 666 Fifth Avenue, New York, New
York 10103.*

PRINTED IN THE UNITED STATES OF AMERICA

O   0 9 8 7 6 5 4 3 2 1

To my own Joe, who understands because—bless his heart—he's as crazy
as I am. And to my children: Tami—
my firstborn, my friend; Bubba—my
beloved only son, my resident pain in
the neck; and Amanda—my miniature
dictator, my joy

One

"... and although the men are not known to be armed, official sources advise that they should be considered dangerous. The escape of the prisoners yesterday has aroused speculation about the adequacy of the county facilities, renewing interest in the upcoming bond issue. In a recent interview, County Commissioner Henderson warned—"

"Jeffrey Fisher, I thought I told you not to bring that radio!" Abby turned around to look down at her ten-year-old son in exasperation.

"It's not mine. It's Chuck's," he protested, holding the now-silent portable behind his back before surreptitiously passing it to a boy standing beside him. "And anyway, you should be glad we have it. Those murderers could be hiding in the trees watching us right now."

"They aren't murderers," Abby Fisher said irritably, feeling her gaze drift uncontrollably over her shoulder into the surrounding tangle of underbrush. "They held up a grocery store."

"They could have killed people that nobody knows about." His voice had dropped to an ominous whisper and now a gleam of excitement appeared in his hazel eyes. "And they're desperate. You know what they say about desperate men."

"No, I don't. And neither do you, so button up. You're scaring Harrison."

"He's not scared." He darted a glance over his shoulder at a chubby blond boy who stood on the narrow path with his hand pressed to his mouth. "Are you, Harry? Why, if those guys are sneaking around in the woods, we can take care of 'em, can't we, Harry? We'll just—" He broke off abruptly when Harrison bounded into the trees. "Holy cow," he muttered under his breath, then turned to smile innocently at his mother. "I don't think Harry feels too good."

"Jeff, I could strangle you," she said, glaring at him as she rushed to where the blond boy was leaning weakly against a tree. She pulled a handkerchief from the pocket of her khaki shorts and helped him wipe his mouth, then looked down at his pale face, her gray-green eyes softening in sympathy. "Do you feel better now, Harrison?"

"Yes, ma'am." He turned to look at the small cluster of boys standing on the trail. "Mrs. Fisher, don't be mad at Jeff. I don't mind if he teases me."

"How could you not mind?" she asked in bewilderment. "You throw up every time he does it."

"I throw up all the time anyway," he said reasonably. "And Jeff calls me Harry," he added, as though that explained everything.

"If you say so," she said doubtfully, wondering once again if she would ever understand boys. Her thirteen-year-old daughter's moods and motivations were clear to her—she could remember going through much the same thing herself—but boys were a whole different can of worms, she thought.

"An apt description if I ever heard one," she murmured in amused exasperation. Heaving a sigh of admitted self-pity, she distractedly pulled at a clump of undergrowth, letting all but one leafy vine slide through her fingers as she followed Harrison back to where the other boys waited.

If Don were alive, perhaps he could have helped her delve into the intricacies of the male mind. But then again, probably not. As good a man as Don had been, he still had believed children were to be fed and clothed and then ignored until they were old enough to make sense.

The subject was academic anyway, she decided with a shrug. She was on her own and would have to continue winging it as she had for the last three years. Hopefully, by the time Jeff figured out that his mother had no idea how to be a parent to a mysterious male, he would be too old to take advantage of the fact.

Smothering a groan as she picked up her backpack, she gave the snickering boys a squelching glance and motioned for them to continue their hike.

Jeff caught up with her before she had gone more than a few feet, looking up at her hesitantly. "Mom—"

"Don't talk to me," she said, glancing down at him from the corners of her eyes. "Although I've stopped considering smothering you in your sleep, I'm still thinking real hard about leaving you on the steps of an orphanage with a note pinned to your shirt."

"But Mom—" he repeated urgently.

"Jeff." She stopped slapping the weed she still carried against her leg and shook it at him sternly. "I'll talk to you when you've apologized to Harris—er, Harry," she amended, "and not before."

"Okay," he said doubtfully. "I just wanted to tell you that you're carrying poison ivy."

She stared at the leafy stem in her hand, then dropped it with comical haste. "I knew that," she lied, wiping the palms of her hands on her shorts in agitation. "I just don't happen to be allergic to it." She fidgeted uncomfortably as she felt an overpowering itch between her shoulder blades. "Now get back in line with the others."

Why her? she wondered helplessly. Had she ever once marched in a women's lib demonstration? Had she ever burned even one of her bras? No. She freely admitted that there were some things that were better left to men. And taking a bunch of undersized storm troopers camping was one of them.

"Mrs. Fisher," said a breathless, urgent voice behind her. "Mrs. Fisher, I've got to—" The tall, redheaded boy broke off, giving her a pained look.

She sighed. "Okay, Chuck. Go behind that tree. And watch out for the poison ivy. It's all over the place." She glanced back at the others, shooting a warning glance at Jeff who was rolling his eyes in youthful contempt. "We'll stop here for a while, guys. If anyone else feels the . . . um . . . call of nature, take care of it now or forever hold your peace."

Removing her heavy pack, she sat down under a tall tree. Then she carefully inspected the area and surreptitiously rubbed her back against the rough bark of the tree while she plotted the demise of one Harrison Woodall, Senior—friend, employer, and all-around fink.

She could see him now as he had sat in the living room of her small frame home, smiling benignly at her. "It'll be good for the boys," he'd said. "Get them back to nature for a couple of weekends a month. And it'll be especially good for Jeff. The fathers will take turns teaching them about the outdoor life," he'd added, then moved in for the kill. "Jeff needs more contact with men, Abby."

So where were those men now? she fumed. Suddenly they were all too busy to spare a weekend. And guess who got stuck with the job? The only person in nine counties who couldn't tell the difference between boxwood and hollyhock.

She reached up to push her golden brown hair back from her forehead, then lifted it away from her perspiring neck to catch a cooling breeze. This was definitely not what she had envisioned for her summer vacation. For the three months school was out she had planned on doing her best to avoid anyone under the age of thirty. She had—

"You did too! I saw you." The angry young voices signaled that her break was over. It was time to move on before full-scale war broke out.

"Honest, it wasn't me," Jeff was saying as she approached. "There really was something out there. I saw the bushes move and I heard a noise that sounded kinda like a moan. I bet it was those—"

"Jeff!" Pulling him away from the group, she leaned down and hissed in his face, "Not one more word. Do you understand?"

"But Mom, I really heard something. I was just—"

"I know exactly what you were doing and if you say anything more about those prisoners, I'll tie you to a tree and pick you up on our way back. Understand?"

He grinned good-naturedly, obviously unaffected by the threat. "Okay. I'll keep quiet . . . but I'll keep my eyes open, just in case."

"Jeff . . ." she began warily, not trusting the look in his eyes, but he had already turned back to the others.

She glanced over to where they all stood. Then her eyes narrowed as a feeling of something not quite right began to nag at her. Counting heads quickly, she realized she was one boy short of the five she had begun with.

"Okay, who's missing?" she asked, keeping her voice carefully casual.

"It's Brian," Chuck volunteered. "He had to go."

"He's had plenty of time for that." Her mouth went dry with fear as the possibilities began to hit her. "Which way—"

"Here I am, Mrs. Fisher."

They all turned to watch the stout boy approaching slowly, his hands filled with trailing vines and weeds he had zealously pulled up by the roots.

"My mother said I should learn the names of plants this weekend," he explained, thrusting his prizes into her face. "What are they?"

"We don't have time to identify them right now, Brian," she hedged, avoiding Jeff's knowing look. "We have to push on to the lake before it gets dark. And listen, all of you." She glanced around at her adopted brood. "*Nobody* leaves the group alone from now on."

"My father made us use the buddy system when he took us two weeks ago," Scott, a tall, thin boy, told Abby.

"That makes good sense," she said, smiling. Then when they got lost she would be rid of two of them instead of just one, she thought sarcastically.

Aloud she said, "I think we'll try that. Scott, you walk with Chuck. Brian will stay with Jeff—who will tell him the names of all those plants as we walk. And Harry can walk beside me. Now, let's get moving before"—she paused dramatically—"the tenebrous shadows of eventide obscure our boulevard through the weald."

She took in their comically blank stares with smug satisfaction, then translated. "Before it gets too dark to see the trail."

Abby chuckled softly as she heard the grumbled comments from the ranks. "Teachers," was muttered with rich disgust by several. And the airy, "I knew that," from her son was an echo of her own fib earlier, informing her that he knew she was trying to pay them back for making her feel so inadequate.

Leading them forward, she tried to keep the pace brisk and steady, but the last quarter mile to the lake seemed to take forever. As hard as she tried to force herself to be sensible, she couldn't get her mind off the radio report about those escaped prisoners. To make matters worse, she was plagued by the eerie sensation of being watched, and her eyes kept wandering to the trees lining the trail.

The large, rough-looking man watched from the shadows as the small group continued walking toward the lake. Ducking quickly behind a tree, he stood motionless when Abby looked his way, her golden brown hair picking up the stray sunshine filtering through the trees. He wondered if he should make his move now, while they were still in the thick woods. Then he thought of the commotion the five boys would make. No, now was not the time. A slow smile spread across his irregular features and his dark eyes began to take on a strange look of anticipation. He would wait until dark, until the boys were asleep.

Yes, he thought as he began to move in a roughly parallel line beside the trail, tonight will be better. He would wait.

When they finally reached the chosen spot—a small clearing on the east side of the lake—Abby heaved a sigh of relief. She wanted to drop full-length onto the grass and not move for at least two years. The sun was already only a vivid orange glow on the horizon, though, and she knew that if they were going to have a camp fire, they would have to gather the wood now, before the last rays of the sun were lost.

She set the boys to gathering dry wood, making sure they all stayed within sight, then bent to pick up some twigs to use for kindling. As Jeff moved to her side to pick up a larger branch, she glanced over at him irritably.

"Tell me again why we walked three miles

through the woods when the road comes to within five hundred feet of here. Tell me again and say it loud so I can hear it over my screaming feet and my wincing nerves."

"This is supposed to be a hiking and camping club," he explained patiently. "You can't call five hundred feet a hike."

"I got my legs all scratched up and could possibly come down with the only case of terminal poison ivy in the history of Dannen county because of *semantics*?"

"I told you not to wear shorts," he said firmly before moving away to dump the log on the growing pile of wood. He grinned openly when he heard Abby's muttered curses that—in a more just world—would have turned him into a frog.

After a few minutes she called a halt to the eager gatherers, then picked several good-sized branches from a mound that would have done justice to a Guy Fawkes celebration. Ignoring the boys' numerous suggestions on how to light a fire—including one that involved buffalo hide and a hollow log—she used her lighter to get a medium-sized camp fire going just as the shadows began to surround them.

Instead of settling down to rest beside the fire, Abby took one look at the faces of her crew and went scrambling in her backpack for marshmallows. Maybe if she kept their mouths full, they wouldn't . . .

But it was no use. The marshmallows disappeared with disgusting swiftness, she thought. The small group stared blankly when she suggested with overly enthusiastic joviality that they hit the sack early. And they looked at her with the pity reserved for simpleminded adults when, in pure desperation, she proposed singing camp songs.

There was no way out of it. She should have known it was useless from the beginning. The perverse little fiends were going to tell ghost stories.

Even though she tried very hard not to listen, Abby was soon drawn against her will into the traditional pastime. Their ability to savor nuances and throw in artistically gruesome details amazed and horrified her. How could seemingly normal, well-adjusted boys turn into bloodthirsty little ghouls at the drop of a hat? she wondered weakly.

She managed to keep her poise through the Lady of the Lake and a much-embellished version of the Legend of Sleepy Hollow, but when they began the Madman With The Rusty Hook Where His Hand Should Be, she had to grit her teeth to keep from flinching at the rustling sounds coming from the woods behind them and the eerie prickling on the back of her neck.

"And it was when these guys were on a camping trip"—Jeff looked around the camp fire with an evil smile—"just like ours, that the Madman was seen for the last time. They went into the woods just like all the others"—his voice dropped to a sinister whisper—"and never came out again. The next morning, when the police searched the woods, they couldn't find a trace of them. Then, just when they were ready to give up the search, one of them looked up at a tree and there, stuck in the trunk about *twenty* feet off the ground, was the Rusty Hook . . . with blood still dripping—"

He cut off his story abruptly, then yelped,

"Whoops! There he goes again!" as Harry dived into the shadows with Abby close behind him.

When he had finished being sick, Abby pulled Harry down beside her on a weathered log. They sat in companionable silence for a while. Then she glanced down at his pale face. "Why do you come on these trips, Harry?" she asked gently.

"I like camping," he said, then added, his voice slightly woeful, "Besides, Dad started the club for me. I think he thought it would make me tougher."

"What about your mother? Surely she doesn't like the idea of your spending every other weekend throwing up."

"Oh, I don't tell her," he said hastily. "She thinks I grew out of it . . . and if I told her, she wouldn't let me come anymore."

"Is it that important to you?"

"Well, since I only get sick if I'm excited or scared, I figure that if I keep coming, I'll get used to it. It works like that, you know. I used to throw up every time Chuck punched me in the nose. Now I just bleed," he added proudly.

She sat watching him for a moment, a peculiar lump of emotion in her throat. Then she said quietly, "Harry, I think you're just about the bravest boy I've ever met."

As he glanced at her from the corners of his eyes, he seemed to be trying to decide whether she was making fun of him or was simply a little strange. "Mrs. Fisher," he whispered suddenly, "do you suppose one of those escaped convicts has a Rusty Hook Where His Hand Should Be?"

"Of course not," she scoffed, then cleared her throat and stood up hastily to usher him back to the camp fire. "I'll bet those men have already been caught . . . and that story about the Rusty Hook has been going around for a hundred years. It's just a silly story."

Trying very hard to believe her own assurances, she finally succeeded in herding the group into their sleeping bags, telling herself that there was a campground with a guard not two hundred feet away. Somehow it didn't help.

Settling down on a nearby stump with her back to the fire, Abby lit one of her infrequent cigarettes in the hope that it would relax her. She sat listening silently as the excited whispers of the boys turned into the even breathing of sleep.

The sounds of the night creatures and the velvety warmth of the air around her began to work their soothing magic at last, and she found to her amazement she was almost content. She stared with appreciation at the spectacular blanket of stars and felt the last of her knotted nerves unwind.

Friday is over, she thought with a sigh. Now if only she could make it through the rest of the weekend with her life and sanity intact. But maybe that was asking too much. She would probably have to settle for coming out of it alive.

As she thought of the two days to come she shifted uneasily, some of her contentment dissolving. It seemed unbelievable that supposedly responsible parents should trust her with the safety of their children for a weekend in the wilds. Did being a high school English teacher and mother of two automatically qualify her as an outdoor expert?

Principal or no, Harrison was going to feel the sharp side of her tongue for this one. How was she going to fake her way through fishing and exploring and whatever other woodsy things they had planned for the next two days? She couldn't possibly handle it alone.

I need help, she moaned silently.

Then, as though some mischievous god had heard her wordless plea, a shadow fell across the ground in front of her. And unfolding from the huge, shapeless mass was a menacing extension . . . the end twisted fiendishly in the shape of a hook!

Two

Abby jerked upright to free her feet for a hasty exit, then stood paralyzed as her shoulder was caught in a grip of iron. Crazy visions of a giant man wearing a striped prison suit, grasping a ball and chain with a Rusty Hook Where His Hand Should Be careened through her mind. And when she felt her body being slowly but inescapably turned, her only semilucid thought was—if it has eyes, go for them. She had already raised her hand to strike when a voice penetrated her terror.

"Abby! Are you deaf? Why didn't you answer me?"

She stared at the shadows the dying fire cast on the face of her attacker, then whispered hoarsely, "Joe?"

The face before her was not exactly one to inspire confidence on a dark night. His large, crooked nose—which had obviously been broken several times—looked as though the Lord hadn't been able to decide which way he wanted it to go. And the effect of the scar that dipped down into one heavy eyebrow was in no way softened by his neatly trimmed, gray-flecked black hair. The tight

Levi's and faded sweatshirt he wore might have looked casual on another man, but on Joe Gilbraithe they merely served to emphasize the iron strength that had made him famous. There was a toughness about him that at once repelled and attracted. But he was familiar . . . and human. And right at the moment, that was all that seemed to matter.

As she felt the adrenaline seep out of her system, Abby began to sink weakly back to her former position. Then suddenly she changed her mind and straightened to kick him viciously in the shin, inhaling in vengeful satisfaction when she heard his grunt of pain.

"What the hell was that for?" Joe asked, gazing at her warily as he rubbed his injured leg.

"It was either that or throw a screaming fit," she explained with a shrug as she took her seat on the stump. "I figured you'd rather have a sore leg."

"You could be right." He grinned reluctantly as he settled on the ground beside her. "Why was either one necessary?"

"Hooks," she said, turning her eyes sideways to look at him in disgust. "Bloody hooks."

For a moment he stared at her as though trying to figure out the best way to deal with a mental case; then, in the light of the flickering camp fire, she saw a spark of interest grow in his eyes.

"Oh, *those* bloody hooks," he said in comprehension. "You mean I missed the ghost stories? I guess I should have stayed earlier instead of leaving to have dinner."

"Earlier?" His offhand comment jolted her upright. "What do you mean, earlier? How long have you been here?"

"I caught up with you on the trail about a half mile from the lake." He stared at her slowly narrowing eyes and added hastily, "Now don't get all huffy. I wasn't spying on you."

She took a deep breath, then said through clenched teeth, "You were there, watching us, crashing around in the underbrush, giving me a nervous rash because I thought desperate criminals were following us?"

He quickly drew his legs out of kicking range, still watching her closely as he nodded with cautious amusement.

Drawing in her breath slowly and deeply, she strove to remain calm. "Why? Why didn't you just say 'Here I am'? The boys would have been thrilled to death."

"Yes, I know." His soft reply went a long way toward cooling her heated blood. "Because I'm a big-shot football star. That's why I didn't say anything. I'm sorry, maybe I was wrong."

"I don't understand."

"You're supposed to be in charge," he said simply, with an offhand shrug. "If I had arrived just then, it would have disrupted things completely."

Abby stared at him in confusion, then said slowly, "You were afraid you would undermine my authority with the boys?" At his confirming nod, she added in amazement, "You really are a nice person, aren't you?"

"Uh-huh, I am," he said, modestly bowing his head. Then he looked up and grinned. "I'm cute too."

Laughing softly, she said, "So, why are you here? Surely you didn't come all the way out here just to scare me out of my wits?"

His laugh joined hers and the low, rumbling sound was somehow comforting as it drifted through the dark trees. "As a matter of fact I didn't."

He leaned his back against a nearby log. As he rested his hands on his bent knees, looking very relaxed—almost content—her heart took up a strange Morse code beat in response, and she had to make an effort to catch his next words.

"Harrison sent me to help you with the kids."

Abby stared straight ahead, absorbing the meaning of his quiet statement. After a moment she fished another cigarette out of her pocket and lit it in thoughtful silence, then turned to gaze at him with narrowed eyes. "Oh, he did, did he?"

When she caught him staring at her, she gave him her best smile and said sweetly, "Now why do you suppose Harrison would do that, Joe?"

"Because he knows I like kids and he knew . . . thought you might need help," he explained, his voice puzzled. "Do you resent that? Would you rather go it alone?"

"Oh, no. I freely admit that I need help. I didn't want to be in charge of this little safari in the first place." She paused, throwing a calculating glance in his direction. "Didn't it occur to you and Harrison that the other parents might object to the two of us—unattached as we both are—being out here alone for the weekend?"

"Is that what's bothering you?" he asked, relief and amusement plain in his voice. "Don't worry about that. He called all the parents and they gave their full approval."

"The plot thickens," she murmured, grinding out her cigarette. "Tell me, Joe. In the month that

you've been in town"—she met his eyes squarely—
"how many people have told you what a good cook I
am and what a great personality I have and what a
wonderful mother I am?"

Deep grooves formed between his brows as he
gazed at her thoughtfully. Then suddenly he slid to
an upright position, his eyes widening. "Good
grief! You're right." Abby had to stifle a giggle at
the horror in his voice. "Have they been pulling the
same thing on you?"

She nodded emphatically. "Oh, yes. I think I'll
scream if I hear one more person tell me what a
good catch you are. 'But Abby,' " she mimicked,
" 'he's famous . . . and *so nice*. He'd make such a
wonderful father for Jeff and Brennie. Just look at
the work he's done with the Special Olympics.' And
in case I have a mercenary streak, they all tell me
how well your Shrimp Shacks are doing." She
lifted her eyes comically to heaven, then rested her
chin on her fists and looked toward him in exasperation. "Then comes the grabber. 'He does shaving cream commercials,' for heaven's sake!"

Suddenly she began laughing uncontrollably
as her ready sense of humor came to the fore. "The
funniest part is that the commercials seem to
impress them more than anything else."

"Antiperspirant," he muttered. Then seeing
her quizzical glance, he added, "Not shaving cream
. . . antiperspirant."

She grinned at the disgruntled look on his
face. "I'm sorry, but all you jocks look alike to me."

"Thanks." He chuckled. "I noticed in that list
of my virtues an accounting of my extreme good
looks was noticeably absent."

"Oh, they mentioned your looks," she said, trying with difficulty to keep a straight face. "Every one of them classified you as . . . uh . . . masculine." She burst out laughing and reached out to touch his arm in an invitation to share the absurdity. "And they said it just like that," she gasped, her laughter gaining momentum as he joined her, "with a long pause preceding the word."

Abby smothered her laughter behind both hands when one of the boys began to stir. When she was calmer, she stared for a moment at Joe's unusual, thoroughly male face and murmured thoughtfully, "Actually, I think you're very attractive. I haven't figured out why yet, but I do."

"Animal magnetism?" he suggested hopefully, regaining his comfortable position against the log.

"That's possible," she admitted, then leaned forward to rest her chin on her hands as she studied his face thoughtfully. "But it's more likely because I find you a fascinating paradox."

"Fascinating I'll admit to, but how a paradox?"

"You've got a neck," she explained. "I thought all football players were neckless."

He grinned appreciatively. "That's only the linemen. Quarterbacks are allowed to have necks."

Why hadn't she seen before what a nice person he was, she wondered as they sat in the soft, enveloping warmth of the evening, a companionable silence growing between them.

After a while he inhaled deeply, breathing in the fragrant aroma of the dying camp fire as he glanced around at the sleeping boys. Then he said reluctantly, "What are we going to do? Should I leave?"

"Oh, no. Don't you dare," she said hastily. "The boys were already beginning to see through my attempts to fake it. You'll just have to learn how to handle our well-meaning friends. Now that you're onto their scheme, you just smile and agree with everything they say . . . then forget about them. I've been doing it for years."

"You mean they make a habit of matchmaking?"

"A habit?" she said dryly. "They make it their life's work. For some reason unmarried people make married people nervous. It's like two loose ends that need tying up. I've been a widow for three years, and for two and a half of those I've been dodging 'Have I got a man for you!' It was irritating at first, but I've learned to live with it."

"I don't see how you can treat it so lightly. It was a rotten trick for them to pull." His voice was disgruntled and more than a little annoyed.

"Sending you out here?"

"No, the matchmaking thing," he said heatedly. He stared up at the stars, then added, "I had"—he hesitated momentarily as though searching for the right word—"plans of my own."

"Plans?"

"Uh-huh," he confirmed, then swung his eyes back to her, giving her a swift, all-encompassing examination. "Plans."

"Oh, *plans*," she said in dawning comprehension, then shook her head in sympathy. "Put a cramp in your style, did they? Well, just to ease your mind, you picked the wrong target. I wouldn't have succumbed to your charm. So really, you should thank them for saving you the time and trouble."

He leaned his head back against the smooth, weathered surface of the log, then shifted his eyes to study her intently. "Is that right?" he murmured, a purposeful strength entering his voice.

"Uh-oh." She chuckled as she shook her head ruefully. "Now I've aroused your hunting instincts. I honestly didn't intend to challenge you. So you can take that gleam out of your eyes," she added hastily.

He continued to stare at her, this time with a slightly puzzled expression. "You're very casual about the male-female thing, aren't you?"

"I could never see any reason for getting so intense about it," she said, shrugging. "When you spend nine months of the year watching hundreds of giggling Mata Haris vamping pubescent Don Juans and vice versa, it makes you want something more straightforward and less nerve-racking. I believe in saying what I think, as long as it's not deliberately unkind."

"And you don't think it's unkind to tell me you have no intention of letting me make love to you?"

Her eyelids drifted down as she drew in a sharp breath. "When will I learn to keep my mouth shut?" Abby muttered to herself. She opened her eyes to stare at him with wry amusement, adding, "You said that because of what I said about plain speaking . . . right?"

He gave her a slow, sensual smile. "As long as I know the rules, I try to stick to them."

"That's . . . admirable of you." She swallowed, making a vain attempt to keep her composure. "But since the game was called off, I don't think we need to worry about the rules."

"Oh?" He sat up and somehow his face came very close to hers. "No rules?"

"What I mean . . ." She gave a nervous little

laugh. "I mean that the rules for friendship are different from the rules for—"

"A love affair?" he offered. "A seduction?"

She fell silent, momentarily distracted by the sexual tension that had suddenly begun to grow between them. "Seduction's a nasty word," she said finally, sitting up to rest her chin in the palms of her hands. "Don't you think so?" She swung her head sideways to gaze inquiringly at him. "Seduction implies that the woman is stupid—or weak—enough to be persuaded to do something she really doesn't want to do or that she knows is wrong." She shook her head emphatically. "No, I don't believe in that word. If an adult female makes love with a man, it's because she wants to . . . even if she won't admit it to herself."

"It's an interesting hypothesis," he said softly. "We could"—he ran a single finger up the line of her calf to her bare thigh—"put it to the test."

"Oh, Lord," she whispered with comic, but very real, alarm. "You've turned it on full force now, haven't you?" She wrapped her arms around her waist as a shiver of awareness shook her body, then added in a thin voice, "I thought you'd decided the busybodies of Bardle had put a monkey wrench into your amorous plans?"

"I changed my mind." He chuckled softly and the sound started the shivers running in the opposite direction. "It could add a whole new dimension to the game. Don't you realize that practically everything you've said tonight has only intrigued me more?"

"Don't be intrigued," she said helplessly. "Whatever I said, I take it all back."

"Too late. You said you can't see anything to

get so intense about—which makes me very much want to show you just how much there really is to get intense about. The fact that the whole town will be watching avidly will merely be a test of my ingenuity."

She gave a startled laugh, then said, "I think it's at this point that I'm supposed to play the outraged female and say something trite and totally meaningless like 'How dare you' or 'Of all the nerve.'"

"Yes," he agreed softly as he examined her face with sharp eyes that were filled with speculation. "And I wonder why you're not . . ."

He wasn't the only one who was wondering, she admitted silently, then stood and looked down at him. "Now would be an excellent time for me to make my exit," she said cautiously. "Your . . . um . . . game sounds a little out of my depth." She grinned suddenly. "But, if nothing else, it should be very interesting watching you dodge my dear friends and neighbors."

She could still hear his soft laughter as she crawled inside her sleeping bag moments later. Lying there watching the stars, her mind was taken over completely by the incredible conversation that had just taken place.

Now why wasn't I spitting mad when he made that outrageous announcement? she wondered. What kind of emotional stage was she going through that would allow her to calmly accept Joe's declaration of his intention to stalk her as though she were a trophy elk?

Perhaps she'd accepted it simply because he *had* been so open about it. Open and honest herself, she was wary—and perhaps a little contemptuous—of devious people. And maybe, just maybe, she was more than a little intrigued herself.

Intrigued and flattered. Though she would certainly never have admitted it to Joe. Nor would she admit that at her first meeting with him a month earlier, she had found herself very much attracted to this strangely magnetic man. Something had happened that first night that she didn't understand. An unfamiliar emotion had grown inside her, an emotion that made her just a little uneasy.

She'd tried to keep in mind that, until recently, he had been seen by millions every Monday night during the football season in his job as color commentator. She'd tried to convince herself that she was feeling the same fascination any average person would feel upon meeting a celebrity.

But somehow it had seemed like more than that and, just to be on the safe side, she had carefully ignored the attraction. He had enough people in town chasing him; she'd be damned if she would add her name to the list.

Secretly, of course, she was just as excited about having the retired quarterback in their small town as everyone else. There was apparently some sort of tie between Harrison and Joe, since Joe was here at her employer's request. For one school year only. And in that time, he had promised, he'd produce a winning football team.

Abby rolled over in her bag and smothered a chuckle as she thought of the famous Joe Gilbraithe coaching a team with a thirteen-year losing streak behind them. And not only that, but also teaching history! That should certainly shake up the county. Until now the Bardle Bulldogs had been merely a symbol of incompetence.

Joe had said he could change that. And Abby believed that if anyone could pull it off, he could. He hadn't been boasting when he had made the statement, but had exuded a quiet self-assurance that was much more believable.

That same self-confidence had been there when he'd talked of pursuing her, she knew. And although she would never admit it aloud, her summer had suddenly taken on a new sparkle.

Not that she would consider an affair, she assured herself. That was out of the question. Considering Abby's position in the small town, it was very fortunate that she had adjusted so well to doing without sex.

After Don's death, remaining strong for Jeff and Brennie's sake had postponed Abby's own bout with grief, but when she had finally managed to get over the shock and the dreadful sense of loss, she had found to her surprise that she could adjust quite well to being single. She was a healthy woman with healthy appetites, but fortunately those appetites seemed to have vanished at some point after her husband's death.

Teaching at the local high school and being mother to two imaginative children took all of her time and energy, anyway, leaving her no time for loneliness or self-pity. And, after a while, she realized she was content with her life. It brought fulfillment and a kind of peace.

She grinned. She certainly didn't need the complication of Joe Gilbraithe—battered, world-weary, reeking of blatant, masculine sensuality—in her life. No, she didn't need it. But, world-weary or not, being pursued by a man as attractive and intelligent as Joe promised to make this one of her more memorable summers.

As for the unfamiliar sensations he provoked in her, she had not reached the age of thirty-seven without learning to control her feelings. Heaving a smug sigh, she rolled over and at last settled down to sleep.

Joe folded his hands behind his head and listened to Abby shifting restlessly in her sleeping bag. He grinned as he thought of the way she had reacted to his deliberately provocative announcement.

What a surprise and joy she was, he thought. The moment he had seen her a month ago he had sensed that she was different. He was only now discovering just how different.

When she had walked into the welcome party given for him by Harrison, the whole room had seemed to come to life. As she'd made her way across the room, her hair shining like antique gold in the bright light, she was stopped by each group she encountered on the way. It had taken her half an hour to traverse the room. And half an hour of watching her was all he had needed to become thoroughly entranced.

Perhaps that special feeling she generated everywhere was the reason he had missed the matchmaking efforts behind the comments made by almost everyone he met. It had somehow seemed natural that they should all praise her. She was different . . . special . . . unique. All the things needed to capture his imagination. Capture it and hold it.

Everyone else in the small town treated Joe like a celebrity. But not Abby. She had treated him like an ordinary human being at that very first meeting. That, and the fact that she had the most gorgeous pair of legs he had ever seen, had made him decide with an uncharacteristic lack of caution that he would get to know her—and her legs— much better before the summer was over.

Of course, he thought, rolling over on his side, the fact that the small community would be watching his every move might slow down his progress. Everyone in town seemed to be in love with Abby. And, as a result, extremely protective of her.

Even the people he could swear were not matchmakers smiled when they mentioned her name. He had never in his life met anyone who provoked that reaction. Usually someone as attractive and popular as Abby brought out jealousy in those less fortunate. But he had seen not one hint of that from the people in Bardle. Loving Abby seemed to be universal in the small town. That fact alone would have intrigued him.

And Joe was definitely not a man to let a few stumbling blocks get in the way of what he wanted. He grinned suddenly as a burst of exhilaration shot through him. It was anticipation, he decided. Because the truth was that Joe thrived on opposition—the more, the better.

He had come to Bardle to make his peace with the past—old debts, old memories, memories from a different time, a different world. But in the meantime he had been presented with all the makings of a very interesting summer and he intended to take full advantage of them.

Three

Abby groaned and pulled the top of the sleeping bag over her head. Too much sunshine. Too much noise. She didn't ask that the day pamper her with a gentle awakening, but did it have to start out with such a bang? she asked silently.

"Hello." Joe's greeting was muffled by the down-filled nylon sack that was pulled tightly around Abby's ears. "Are you in there?"

"No." Her voice was faint, but uncompromising.

Even within her cocoon, she could hear his chuckle clearly. For the love of Pete, she thought irritably, no one has the right to chuckle at this time of the morning.

"Abby," he coaxed softly, giving the nylon a gentle tug. "If you'll come out, I'll give you coffee and breakfast."

"Coffee?" She eased her death grip on the sleeping bag and lifted it away from her face so that a slice of sunshine slid in. Suddenly her nostrils began to twitch. Intrigued against her will, she pulled the bag down just enough to expose her eyes. "Is that bacon I smell?"

His brown-almost-black eyes sparkled, deep grooves of amusement appearing at the corners as he nodded silently and rocked back to sit on his heels.

She pulled herself up to a sitting position, knowing that her hair would be in a wild tangle of curls after a night in the damp air, but unable to summon up one ounce of vanity so early in the day. Giving him a suspicious look, she grumbled, "I didn't bring bacon. What did you do—rope a wild boar and roast it over an open pit?"

"Almost," he said, grinning. "The boys and I drove to the store while you were asleep."

"Drove?" Suddenly she was wide awake. "Where's your car?"

He nodded to the right and she jerked her head in that direction. Sure enough, she could see his cream-colored Buick through the trees.

"Do you mean to tell me"—she turned her head back to stare at him in indignant disbelief—"that I walked through thirty miles of hostile territory with five sticks of dynamite whose sole purpose in life was to see me come to an untimely—and preferably unpleasant—end, when you—you—" she sputtered, "you drove here and walked a back-breaking ten feet to reach us?"

"Oh . . . you awake, Mom?"

Twisting her head around, she speared her only son with a look that condemned simply because he was male.

"I was beginning to think a rattler had crawled in there with you in the middle of the night," he said with cheerful unconcern. "They're attracted to body heat, ya' know."

As Jeff walked away to join the other boys,

Abby sighed. "Why do I get the impression that I'm a failure as a mother because I wasn't bitten by a snake last night? Somehow he makes me feel that if I really cared, I would be all black and swollen this morning."

The sound of laughter brought her eyes back to Joe. "And don't think I'm through with you yet. That was a dirty trick."

"Honest, Abby," he assured her, his laughter dying down to an occasional uncontrollable chuckle. "I would have taken them on the trek if I had been here, but I only got back to town yesterday afternoon." He smiled beguilingly. "And I walked much farther last night. I just pulled the car up closer this morning."

She gazed at him with narrowed eyes. "How far?"

"Well . . ."

"How far?" she repeated stubbornly.

He rubbed his jaw thoughtfully. "Five hundred feet," he murmured finally, then nodded emphatically. "Yes, I'd make it a good five hundred feet."

"And you can still walk?" she muttered, giving him a look of feigned astonishment. Then she shrugged, too stiff to ignore his helping hand as she rose. "If my brain hadn't deserted its post, I'd think of some way to get even with you—but since it has, lead me to the coffee and I'll forgive you anything."

"Anything?"

She glanced up as she heard the provocative tone of the murmured word. "Don't press your luck, quarterback. It's too early in the morning for that stuff."

After handing her a cup of coffee, he searched

her face, then closed his eyes for a moment and inhaled slowly, as if he had just thought of something extremely pleasant. "Ah, Abby, the list of things I'm going to teach you just keeps on growing." He opened his eyes to gaze deeply into hers. "It's never too early for 'that stuff.' "

Suddenly there was something in his face and deep in his eyes that took their playful banter out of the realm of fun and games. The air between them grew heavy with a startlingly vibrant sexual tension, causing Abby to draw back warily.

She could feel him watching her as she tried to deal with this new and disconcerting emotion, but she couldn't come up with a flip retort. Not when the game had shifted direction and left her dizzy with the change.

This was not how it was supposed to be, she thought breathlessly. Flirting with Joe, fencing with him verbally, fielding his overt sexual innuendoes—it was all just a pleasant pastime . . . wasn't it?

Before she could carry the uncomfortable thought any further, the boys descended on them. As the moment of acute awareness passed, Abby decided it must have been a figment of her imagination. Joe's face carried not a hint of the earlier sensuality as they ate breakfast.

Later, while she was folding her sleeping bag, the boys began getting their fishing gear together. She silently blessed Harrison's devious nature because it meant that now she didn't have to make a fool of herself by trying to pretend she knew how to fish.

But it seemed her relief had been premature,

because moments later Joe appeared before her carrying not one, but two fiberglass rods.

"You fish with two rods?" she asked hopefully.

"Jeff tells me you can't fish. I'm going to teach you how," he explained, with depressing enthusiasm, she noted.

"No, really, Joe. That's awfully sweet of you, but I've tried and"—she shrugged her shoulders with smug resignation—"I'm hopeless."

"You'll soon get the hang of it." He gave her an encouraging glance as he turned to walk toward the lake.

"But Joe," she protested, hurrying to keep up, "you don't understand. I don't mean I need a little practice. I mean I'm unteachable. I tried for years to cast, but somehow I always managed to land my lure in a tree."

From the sound of his chuckle she gathered he really wasn't weakening, so she tried again.

"Joe," she said firmly, grasping his arm to pull him to a halt. "When Jeff got his first rod and reel for Christmas, he asked me to show him how to cast it." She paused, letting him feel the full impact of her sad tale. "I showed him, Joe . . . and the lure landed in the Christmas tree. That's got to be some kind of sign. You could use me as a divining rod for trees . . . I swear."

He began walking again, obviously unaffected by the strength of her evidence. Then he threw her a glance over his shoulder. "You give up too easily."

She stared at his back and gave a mental shrug. Oh, well, some people had to be shown, she decided. On his head be it.

Her first few casts were deceptively accurate, and it was only after her fourth cast that the inevitable disaster struck. Abby could have sworn that she did nothing different from the first three tries, but the wicked lure had a mind of its own, and while she was staring at the spot where it should have landed, she heard the violent rustle of leaves to her right.

She turned in resignation, knowing beforehand what she would see. Her gaze found a large willow tree and, sure enough, hanging there three feet in the air was the cunning little white devil that was supposed to be enticing a black bass. When she turned to shrug and smile at Joe, the lure dropped the three feet to the water with a splash, leaving her line draped over a tree limb.

"You can't say I didn't warn you," she said, wiggling the tip of her rod innocently.

"How did it get there?" He actually looked bewildered, she noticed, as though she hadn't carefully explained the whole thing to him in advance.

She rested the rod against her shoulder and shrugged again. "If I knew that, I'd be teaching physics or aerodynamics instead of English. I just know it always happens."

The next sequence of events happened so fast, they all seemed to take place at once. She couldn't tell whether she felt the increased pressure of the rod on her shoulder first or if that came after she heard the boys' shouts and saw Joe's eyes widen in astonishment.

She simply knew that Joe and all five boys suddenly rushed toward the lake, simultaneously shouting, "Set the hook!" as they waded in.

"In what?" she gasped as she yanked on the rod and saw the limb that supported her line bow down ominously. As the group reached the tree that grew half-in and half-out of the water, she started to reel vigorously.

The frantic chorus of "Don't reel!" came too late. She had inched the fish out of the water just far enough to get a glimpse of its extreme size when it gave a tremendous shudder, shaking the hook loose, and disappeared into the dark green water. Then all was silent.

Staring down at her feet, Abby tried to ignore the stereophonic splashing sounds that drew slowly nearer. She began to whistle softly under her breath, scuffing the toe of her sneaker in the dirt. But when she saw six pairs of feet surrounding her, she was forced to look up.

She smiled innocently. "That was some fish, huh?"

Joe's lip began to twitch, causing the drops of water that covered his face to quiver in the sunlight. Then, moments later, the seven of them were lying on the grass as laughter overcame them one by one.

"You've got to show me how you did that," Joe gasped, holding his sides.

Groans of "A *lake record*" and the more philosophic "It could only happen to a mother" were heard from the pint-sized, chauvinistic bunch.

Abby was finally beginning to bring her laughter under control when she glanced over at Joe. The T-shirt that was plastered to his muscular chest, the dripping wet cutoff jeans, and the streak of mud on his face combined to set her off again. She rolled over on her side away from the sight of him, then yelped in surprise when she felt herself being lifted to the accompanying cheers of the crowd.

"What are you doing?" she screeched as Joe approached the lake with her in his arms.

He smiled evilly. "What does it look like?"

"Joe . . . let's discuss this." She locked her arms around his neck. "Wait—I thought you were going to beguile me with your winning ways. With an eye to developing a . . . closer relationship in the future."

"Uh-huh," he agreed affably.

"And you really think dunking me in the lake is going to do that?" She tightened her hold on his neck as he waded into the water. "We gotta sit down and have a long talk about your technique, Joe. It leaves a little to be desired."

"Sit down?"

Abby definitely didn't like the gleam she saw in his eyes, but before she could do more than gasp "No!" he sat down with her in his arms.

She remained thoughtfully silent as the warm water seeped through her clothes. Then she turned her head slowly to look up at him. "Now, don't you feel silly?"

Throwing back his head, he gave a shout of laughter. Then, still chuckling, he glanced over his shoulder toward the bank to watch as their appreciative audience slowly dispersed. Suddenly his hand was running slowly up her water-slick thigh.

"I feel something," he said softly, "but it's certainly not silly."

Suddenly Abby became aware that she was pressed firmly against him, her blouse almost no barrier at all in the warm water. His hand running up and down her leg, his hard thighs beneath her, the sensual look of his full, firm lips—which amazingly were now only a breath away—all caused a curious tightening in her chest and an equally strange quickening of her pulse.

"No." His husky whisper brushed softly across her tingling lips. "Not silly at all."

Sliding his hand over her hip and up her ribs, he let it come to rest just below her breast. Somehow the fact that the caress was taking place under water made it overwhelmingly erotic. Abby caught her breath in surprise when she found herself wishing he would raise his hand just the few inches it would take to cover her breast completely.

"Well," she said in a gust of air as she stared at a point far out in the lake. "I guess I'd better get back to the boys . . . I think they're plotting something. When I heard them talking about burning someone at the stake . . . well, I—I just prayed that it wasn't me." She knew she was rambling, but the knowledge didn't slow down her tongue. "Now I think I'd better investigate, and if it's Jeff they had in mind . . . well, if it's Jeff, maybe I'll help gather the wood. . . ."

For a moment it was as though he hadn't heard a word of her breathless monologue, for he kept his arms firmly around her. Then he smiled a slow smile and grasped her by the waist to lift her to her feet. His silent, watchful amusement caused her to pull nervously at the green jungle-print blouse that clung stubbornly to her upper body.

As they walked back to where the boys were, Abby wondered if this thing with Joe was really such a good idea after all. She honestly wasn't interested in an affair. Maybe the way she'd teased him gave him the wrong idea. Perhaps she should make her position clear before things got out of hand, she pondered.

Despite having been married all her adult life, Abby wasn't very experienced in sophisticated games. Yet she knew there were ways to handle these things gracefully. The only problem—and she freely admitted there *was* a problem—was that she liked the attention Joe was paying her. She thoroughly enjoyed being pursued by such an attractive man. And to tell the truth she was curious about the way he made her feel. She had known a good many men in her life, some of them very attractive. But never had she felt the awareness, the exhilaration that filled her when Joe was near.

You can't have it both ways, she warned herself silently. It was an either-or thing. Tonight, she decided. Tonight when the boys were asleep she would talk to him honestly and then see what happened.

But first she had to get through the rest of today, she thought. And judging by the way the boys swarmed eagerly around them as soon as she and Joe walked back to their camp, that wasn't going to be such an easy task. Fortunately the next hour and a half were taken up with cleaning, cooking, and consuming the ones that *didn't* get away.

"Joe, who messed up your leg like that? I bet you didn't let 'em get away with it. I bet you trashed 'em good for hitting you so hard."

Abby glanced up from the crisply fried fish on her plate to give her son a threatening look. When would he ever learn proper manners?

"Jeff," she said grimly when she failed to catch his eye.

Her son stared at her blankly for a moment, then his mouth formed an O of comprehension. "It's impolite to ask personal questions, right?" he said brightly.

Rolling her eyes in exasperation, she threw Joe an apologetic glance.

"No, it's all right, Abby." He chuckled, then looked down at the boys, who were elbowing and shoving each other to sit as close to him as possible. "It wasn't just one person who did this." He indicated the scars on his left leg. "I have the history of my ten years in football carved into my body. It's something you guys better think about before any of you decide to go into pro ball."

He grinned as he saw the lecture having no effect at all, giving Abby a look that seemed to say "At least I tried." "I can see you're going to insist on all the grisly details. Well, take this one." He pointed to a long, thin scar and rubbed it. "I got this one from an operation I had after a Super Bowl game. You remember the one I'm talking about?"

And with those few words he had them in the palm of his hand. As he gave them a blow-by-blow account of his injuries, the group sat open-mouthed and silent.

Later, after he asked the boys to clean up the campsite before they went for a hike, Joe turned to Abby and said softly, "The scars . . . they don't bother you, do they?"

She stared at him in confusion. "Bother me? Why on earth should they bother me?"

"They're not exactly beautiful." He smiled ruefully. "In fact, they're pretty gruesome. It looks like my body has been taken apart, then reassembled by an amateur."

She studied his legs for a moment. "No, they're not beautiful, but unless you were considering a career as a Rockette, I can't see that it's all that important." She smiled. "Of course, you probably won't get any work modeling panty hose on television."

He laughed and sat back, brushing the scars lightly with his callused fingers. Abby clasped her hands tightly around her knees, for suddenly, out of nowhere, came the urge to reach out and touch him herself.

Raising her eyes slowly, she heard him draw in his breath sharply and knew he had recognized the strange yearning that was reflected in her eyes. For a moment they simply sat and stared at each other, and Abby experienced the most complete, astoundingly clear communication she had ever known. Silent, but complete. It was a startlingly exhilarating revelation of a truth she had never guessed existed. How could she have known two minds could really work as one?

It seemed to make a mockery of all the things she had learned over the years about human relationships. And, like all human beings who are faced with the annihilation of their known world, she was suddenly afraid and unsure of herself. She didn't want her comfortable truths tampered with.

Before the strange new sensations could overwhelm her, however, the boys surrounded them, demanding that they begin their hike. She sagged in relief, carefully ignoring the meaningful expression in Joe's dark eyes.

It didn't take long for Abby to convince herself that she was placing too much importance on one look, and time after time in the next two hours she blessed Joe's presence. He had patience with children that she'd very rarely seen in bachelors; more, he treated them as individuals. When they spoke he actually listened to what they were saying. He kept them laughing the whole time, but never let them get out of hand. A look was all it took to calm them down. Before their hike had barely begun, she was wishing she could bottle whatever power he had over them and take it home with her.

Joe glanced over the boys' heads to Abby, who was bringing up the rear. Catching his look, her soft, full mouth curved into a smile and he felt twinges of something so strong, it was almost like pain. But not pain. It was more exciting, more welcome than pain had ever been.

If she were any of the women he had been attracted to in the past, Joe knew he would have been searching for some way to get her alone. But not Abby. Although he very much wanted to be alone with her, for a reason as yet unclear to him he needed to see her with these boys, in these circumstances.

She was totally natural with her charges, never pampering them, but on the other hand never sharp or impatient. Her voice had the same tone when she spoke to him as when she spoke to the boys. It might have seemed a small thing, but it had always irritated him the way some people saved a special voice for speaking to children— sometimes overly sweet, sometimes irritable or condescending—as though children were not quite human, a separate species whose intelligence was questionable.

Abby treated them with the same good manners and respect she accorded everyone she met. It was one more clue to the mystery of the warmth she generated in the people he had met recently, he thought.

Joe chuckled suddenly when she tripped over a root and two of the boys reached out to keep her from falling. They giggled in delight when she bit off a word she didn't want to reach their avid ears and politely thanked them.

"You obnoxious little twerps," she added, laughing with them. "It would thrill you all to see me bruised and bloodied, wouldn't it?"

"It's not that, Mom," Jeff explained. "It's just that we took bets on how long it'd take you to forget we're here and start cussin'."

"Jeffrey Fisher," she said indignantly. "When have you ever heard me use vulgar language?"

He answered without hesitation. "The time you hit your thumb with a hammer helping me build the tree house, the time you broke three fingernails changing a tire, the time Merry tripped you and made you drop a dozen eggs, the time—"

"All right, all right," she said, cutting him off. She glanced at Joe and shrugged her shoulders as she whispered, "The snitch. Who knew he was keeping score?"

As they began to walk again, Abby watched a grin spread over Joe's strong, well-shaped mouth. If she allowed herself, she could become addicted to those lips. They were full and sharply defined, instead of melting indistinctly into the surrounding flesh as some did. The only other man she had ever seen with lips as bold as Joe's was Elvis Presley.

Watch it, she warned herself silently when she saw where her thoughts were leading. She had to remember that she had already decided to warn

Joe off as soon as she had the chance. She stifled a wistful sigh when she found herself wishing that the chance wouldn't come too soon.

Inevitably, though, the day was over and she knew she had to decide how she was going to make her position clear to Joe. As she helped clear away the remains of their dinner, she began to build strong, sensible arguments in her mind.

However, when the time actually came, when the boys had finally settled down without benefit of scary tales thanks to Joe's filling in with old football stories, Abby found herself reluctant to bring it up again.

It was just too comfortable sitting there with him in the soft light of the camp fire. The sexual tension, although still present, was kept carefully below the surface as though by mutual agreement, which made it very difficult to raise the subject without sounding provocative.

"How long have you been teaching?" Joe's deep, quiet voice interrupted her wandering thoughts and seemed to reaffirm her decision to save the serious discussion for later.

"Only since Don's death." She shifted to escape a root that was digging into her hip. "We were married right after high school, so I didn't get the chance to go to college. But when I hit that crazy period most women go through at thirty, I decided I would 'find' myself and get my degree. I had only just graduated when Don had his heart attack."

"And did you? Find yourself, I mean?"

She leaned her head back against a stump and considered the question. "I don't know, but I had a wonderful time trying," she said with a grin. "I

feel a deep dissatisfaction, but won't try to find the cause. I don't understand them so I can't say why . . . maybe fear . . . maybe a poor sense of self-worth." She paused thoughtfully. "And then maybe sometimes you are one thing in one set of circumstances and something different in another."

Abby knew that her theory could apply to herself. When Don was alive she was happy just being his wife and mother to his children. Even when she went back to college, she never really anticipated making a career of teaching; she had merely viewed the experience as necessary to make her a well-rounded person.

If Don had lived she would most likely have been content to spend the rest of her life in that role. But he hadn't lived, and when she was forced to make a new life for herself and her children, she'd found the challenge of her new role as wage earner and single parent exciting and surprisingly rewarding.

Raising her eyes, she found Joe watching her closely with a curiously reflective look in his deep brown eyes. She gave a short, uneasy laugh. "Now on to the trivial. Let's talk about you."

"I love the way you cater to a man's ego!" He chuckled, then said, "My life is an open book. What in particular did you want to know?"

"For starters, you can tell me why you're here. Not that we're not thrilled to have you," she added hastily. "But you've got to admit it seems a little strange. You could coach at any college you wanted. Why a backwater high school team whose motto is: To hell with the Gipper, just win one?"

"As I mentioned yesterday," he said, laughing

softly, "I like a challenge." His laugh grew stronger when she glanced away to avoid his eyes; then his voice grew sober as he added, "But the main reason is that I owe Harrison."

When he didn't carry the explanation further, Abby's curiosity grew unbearably, but good manners prevented her from pushing it any further.

"Come on, let's walk down by the lake." He rose with a grace that seemed at odds with his huge frame, and extended a hand to her.

"The boys—" she began.

"We'll stay close enough to keep an eye on them," he assured her, but she still held back, fidgeting as he sent her a questioning glance.

"The escaped prisoners—"

"Were caught last night before they got two miles away," he finished for her. "I heard it on the radio this morning. Any more objections?"

"No . . . of course not," she mumbled, taking his hand. "I just didn't want them stumbling unawares on the boys; the boys would have massacred them."

He laughed softly and led her down the slope to the edge of the water. The moon was almost full and so close, it looked as though they could just reach out and touch it. Its luminous rays made a seemingly solid pathway across the glassy surface of the dark water.

"Did you ever date any of those men the matchmakers pushed?" His voice was soft and almost reverent, as though he, too, were affected by the ethereal setting.

"A couple in the beginning," she said. "But eventually I decided I'm too selfish to get involved with anyone."

"Selfish?"

She sighed, remembering. "I spent a lot of years compromising. At the time I didn't know that's what I was doing so it didn't bother me. But now I do, and I don't want to compromise anymore. I want to live the way I want to live, without explaining myself or apologizing because it's different from what someone else believes is right." She glanced over at him. "See? Selfish, that's me."

"And you think getting involved precludes leading your own life?"

"Maybe I'd better define what I mean by getting involved." Now was as good a time as any to let him know where she stood, she decided. "I mean emotionally involved. I suppose it's possible for some people to sustain a physical relationship without the emotional entanglement . . . but not for me."

He stopped walking and glanced down at her. "Are you saying you have to be *in* love before you *make* love?"

Bending to pick up a stone, she gave a soft laugh. "You sound skeptical." After making a vain effort to skim the stone across the water, she turned to him. "Actually, that wasn't what I meant to say. I really don't know about that because I've never tried it. It's possible that I could enjoy a casual encounter very much . . . at the time. It's what happens afterward that I'm talking about."

"Afterward?"

"The guilt." She sighed in resignation. "In the spectrum of emotions, there is not one that I'm more familiar with. I don't know if it was the way I was raised, or something in my makeup, but whatever the cause, I've felt enough of it to last a lifetime. I refuse to take on any more."

"What have you done to feel so guilty about?" He sounded amused by her statement.

"Logically, I can say 'nothing.' But logic doesn't help when a person has guilt in her genes," she said wryly. "I've read that it's really a kind of preoccupation with self. I feel guilty about everything . . . as though if I were a better person I could have prevented whatever it is I feel guilty about. And that's supposed to show that I think everything revolves around me . . . a kind of negative ego trip."

"And you believe that?" he asked softly.

"I didn't say I believe it. I simply read it somewhere. I don't know what causes it. Pressure from my parents to be perfect . . . insecurity . . . it doesn't matter. What matters is that I've learned to avoid things I know are going to make me feel guilty. And, given my background and situation, casual sex is guaranteed to bring on a whopper of a guilt trip."

He made no comment as she finished her explanations, and they walked in silence for a while. After a few minutes he stooped to pick up a stone and sent it skipping far out across the lake. Six times at least it bounced on the liquid surface. There must be an extra bone in the mysterious male wrist, she thought with a grimace of sour grapes.

"What are you thinking about?" she asked, disguising her envious sigh.

He stared down at her for a moment, then smiled slowly. "I'm thinking that I have finally found an adversary worthy of my skill."

"I beg your pardon?"

He laughed and sank down to the sand. "That

whole speech was perfect. After all that honesty, what kind of lowlife would persist in trying to make you give in? You never once said that I wouldn't succeed in getting you into bed. You've already said that if a woman sleeps with a man, it's because she wants to . . . thereby relieving me of all blame. But—now comes the clincher—if I succeeded, I would be leaving you to cope with a huge load of guilt."

He laughed again and shook his head. "It was beautiful. I couldn't have done better if I'd worked on that argument for a year!"

She sat down abruptly, then turned to stare at him in amazement. He didn't believe her. He thought it was all a part of the game. She almost took a swing at him; then it suddenly occurred to her that his reaction was just what she wanted. She had been totally honest with him. So, anything that happened now was not her responsibility, she thought. She could enjoy the game with a clear conscience.

"Thank you . . . I think. But how good a move was it if you don't believe me?"

"It stopped me for a few seconds," he allowed generously. "And it warned me to be on my toes. I'll have to spend a lot more time on my strategy than I had planned."

Taking a swing at him really hadn't been that bad an idea, she decided as she gazed at him in part-admiration, part-steaming-indignation. She had never seen anything to match his self-confidence. He had no doubt at all that he would win.

"Of course," he murmured, "that makes the whole thing all the more interesting."

Here it comes, she thought, feeling her pulse

rate quicken in anticipation as his face loomed closer. This was a critical point in the game, and she knew she would have to play it just right. If she gave too much, he would think she was an easy mark. If she gave too little, he might think she wasn't worth the effort.

"This is a very important moment in our relationship," he whispered, echoing her own thoughts. He was so close, she could feel his warm, coffee-flavored breath on her face. "It has to be played exactly right or the whole thing will fizzle out before it begins."

Placing his hand under her chin, he tilted her head. "We can't rush it . . . it has to come slow and easy." He brushed a kiss on the corner of her mouth, then moved to the opposite side. "No demands . . . it has to be freely given," he breathed against her tingling flesh.

Suddenly, as he feathered his lips across hers, then repeated the fairy caress again and yet again, her carefully laid plan went right out of her head, and the wonder of the kiss took its place. She was vaguely aware of a gentle pressure on her shoulders and then of the rough feel of sand through her cotton blouse, but she couldn't seem to pull her concentration away from his firm lips on hers.

Fleeting strokes from the tip of his tongue were a signal for her to part her lips, and she responded automatically, eager to satisfy a burning curiosity to know what other sensations this new assault would bring.

For a moment she lay pliant beneath him, accepting each movement of his tongue as though it were an everyday occurrence instead of the breathless discovery of a new world. Then suddenly she pulled back and stared at him silently with wide, bedazzled eyes.

"You're beginning to understand, aren't you?" His rough whisper carried her a step further into the spiraling wonderland she was finding in his arms. "Just a little more, Abby, and you'll know what all the furor is about."

His index finger began tracing invisible lines down her neck and over her shoulder, then back to her throat and down between her breasts, teasing her . . . tantalizing her with incredible accuracy. Her responsive shiver brought an almost silent laugh of triumph. Suddenly she felt the cool lake breeze touch flesh she was sure should have been covered.

Gazing down, her eyes met the sight of his dark hand against her breast with a pleased shudder of acceptance that would surprise her later.

"You see how your nipples respond to me," he murmured huskily. He passed his fingers fleetingly across the hardened tips in a caress too insubstantial to be anything other than frustratingly arousing. "Your body knows . . . even if you don't."

His tongue flicked down her throat, his fingers brushing against her breasts, but refusing her the final satisfaction of a definite caress. She arched her body with a small moan, trying desperately to press deeper into his hand. She was at the point of begging for his touch, when something like a breeze of reason cleared the sensual mists surrounding her.

This had gone too far, she thought in feeble protest. He was having it all his own way, and if it continued, she would surely forfeit the game. If both sides were to be equally matched, she would have to find a way to make him lose some of his self-confidence.

She had heard his indrawn breath when she arched against him and knew that she would have to take advantage of his momentary weakness before this thing between them got completely out of hand. Sliding her hands up his chest, she grasped his shoulders and lifted her upper torso off the ground to press her breasts against him.

Her aggressive movement seemed to take him by surprise, for he suddenly became still. She lifted her hands to frame his face and, as she applied firm pressure, their positions were reversed. Now he was lying on his back as she leaned over him, her golden brown hair falling on either side of his face.

"We mustn't demand," she breathed against his lips. "We taunt . . ." She pressed a tiny kiss to the corner of his warm, receptive mouth. ". . . then we tease." She moved her mouth to the opposite corner, exploring it gently with her tongue. Her fingers were busy pulling his T-shirt up higher on his chest. "You have to want this as much as I do." She brushed her fingers across his hair-roughened chest, pausing fractionally at the stiff nipples, then moving on with devilish abandon.

She probed deeper with her tongue, grazing his teeth, the roof of his mouth, and circling his eager tongue before withdrawing. Lord, she hoped he didn't know how much she was enjoying paying him back!

When Abby dipped her hand lower to seek out the indentation of his navel just above the low-slung cutoffs, a deep, frustrated groan escaped him and he arched his hips in an urgent, seeking gesture.

Oh, how her fingers ached to linger there on his hot flesh, but she knew she couldn't give up her advantage now. She moved her mouth to his ear, nipping at its intricate structure for a moment before whispering huskily, "Then we call it even and get back to our job as watchdogs."

She was on her feet, buttoning her blouse, before he even had time to comprehend what she had said. For a moment she could concentrate only on keeping her hands from trembling, but as the tense silence drew out, she began to wonder if she had pushed him too far.

Then suddenly he stood up and there was a curious smile playing about his lips. Reaching out, he pulled her close in a swift, crushing hug, swinging her around in a wide circle.

"Dear Lord, Abby," he said, laughter filling his deep voice. "You damn sure know how to make the game interesting. How in hell am I going to survive the wait until the next bout?"

What kind of man was she dealing with? she wondered as they walked arm in arm back to the camp. Always surprising and different . . . and sometimes a little frightening, but definitely intriguing.

Later, as she lay awake staring sightlessly at the starry sky, she felt the stirring of unfamiliar sensations throughout her body—an aching restlessness that was outside her range of experience. She moved fitfully, wondering how she was going to survive the effects of *this* bout, much less the next.

Four

"We're late," Abby muttered, then looked up distractedly from the tangle of clothes in Jeff's suitcase to find her daughter still in the hall, still on the telephone. "Brennie, I told Nonnie and Pop we would be there by three-thirty. That means we have to leave in exactly"—she glanced down at her watch—"five minutes."

When her thirteen-year-old daughter signaled for one more minute, Abby shook her fist threateningly. Turning back to Jeff's suitcase, she sighed in resignation. It was hopeless. She could either use dynamite or let it go the way it was . . . and she had no time to hunt down explosives.

With a crooked smile, she recalled Joe's last words the day before. He had stood by silently as she loaded the boys into her car. Every time she put one boy in the car, another would pop out on the other side. And the whole time Jeff's mouth was going double time.

"You're amazing," Joe had said appreciatively, shaking his head as he watched the leave-taking process. They both knew he could stop the boys' antics with a single word, but by silent agreement,

53

Abby was once again in charge. "Where's your breaking point?" he asked with a grin. "When do you start cracking heads?"

"Cracking heads?" She stopped shoving rebellious young flesh long enough to look at him disdainfully. "We're talking about innocent young boys here." She grinned suddenly. "Besides, I don't get violent in front of company. I will most likely stop a few miles down the road and strangle one of them as an example to the others."

When he'd chuckled in that curious way that sounded like a growl had caught in his throat, she had shivered in response, feeling a peculiar, light-headed moment of loss as she realized it was really the end of the amazing, happy, and somehow enlightening three days. Even though she had felt more than ready to shed the role of camp counselor, she had been—for a stomach-tightening few seconds—almost sorry that their weekend as guard dogs was over.

Joe had handled the chaos of breaking camp with the ease of a born leader, somehow convincing the boys that it wasn't necessary to hike the three miles back to Abby's car. Of course, she had a suspicion that riding in his big, cream-colored Buick had had something to do with their easy compliance.

When they were finally ready to leave, she had been strangely on edge, as though she were waiting for something. But as she'd pulled her station wagon away, not one word of challenge had crossed his lips. She didn't exactly know what she had expected—a whispered word, an intimate glance—anything other than a companionable silence.

It was only after she had dropped the last boy off at his house that the truth had occurred to her. This was part of the game. Joe was keeping her guessing to intrigue her, to keep her mind on him exclusively.

"And doing a damn fine job of it," she admitted ruefully the next day. She pulled her thoughts back to the present and walked through the house on her way to the backyard in search of Number One son.

Not that Joe needed to do anything special to keep her mind on him, she told herself. Her thoughts kept returning to him with the irresistible pull of a compass needle to north.

Abby had awakened this morning with an eagerness to face the day that was unexplainable. She had no idea when she would see Joe again. They had made no plans. She couldn't understand why she was so positive she would see him again, but she was. Oh yes, she would see him, and now, away from the drugging nearness of him, she told herself that she had proven that she could handle an intimate encounter with him. She was even looking forward to the next bout.

This time it was a tug on her slacks that brought her back to the present, and she looked down with eyes that were focused on yesterday.

"Yes, Merry. You're vicious," she said vaguely, trying to pacify the ridiculous ball of fur that was vigorously attacking the hem of her slacks. "A ferocious beast . . . now let go of my pants."

She gave the navy slacks a gentle yank, but it was no use. Even after assuring the golden-haired puppy that she was terrified for her life, he continued to hang on tenaciously, so her progress was slowed down somewhat as she pulled him along behind her across the polished wood floor of the den to the back door.

However, the sight of Merry's master leaning against the fence talking to their next-door neighbor brought Abby a reprieve, and she watched the animal bound across the yard to Jeff.

"Jeff!" she called, shaking her head in exasperation at the sight of her son. "Ten minutes ago you were clean. What happened?"

Glancing down at the grass stains on his thin knees and the dirt on his hands, he opened his mouth to proffer an explanation that she knew from experience would challenge her imagination and waste at least thirty minutes of her precious time.

"Never mind," she said hastily. "You can tell me later. Just go get cleaned up because we will be leaving in two minutes . . . with or without you."

She watched Jeff head for the house, then turned toward the rumble of laughter behind her and gave her neighbor a frustrated glance. "Hush. You know laughing at him only encourages him to be more outrageous."

The old man leaned forward, resting both hands on the gnarled cane that seemed a part of him, and examined her face with ritualistic care. Abby was used to this close scrutiny and gave back look for look, knowing that Eb was getting ready to throw her off balance with his insight and wisdom . . . or to try and shock her with a risque reminiscence.

Tufts of wiry, iron-gray hair poked determinedly from beneath the stained felt hat that was never off his head for long. The fine network of lines etched into his sun-darkened face, rather than suggesting the fragility of old age, gave him a solid, enduring look—like the weathered rocks of the Grand Canyon, she thought.

"Now what makes you think I was laughing at Jeff? Just maybe I was laughing at you, young lady," he said smartly, continuing his surveillance. Sliding one hand down the cane, he raised it to point the worn head at her. "Something's going on," he pronounced knowingly. "There's something bubbling up in your eyes."

Abby glanced away briefly, wondering how much of his intuition was wisdom and how much was pure bull. "You shouldn't laugh at me either, Eb," she hedged. "It encourages me to act more outrageously too."

"You're awful sassy for a widow woman, aren't you?" He eyed her speculatively, then pushed his hat back on his head and murmured thoughtfully, "You've been this town's joy for a long time, Abby. Always making things a little brighter for everyone—old or young—that you come in contact with." He paused and shook his cane in accusation. "But this is new. You got something on the back burner, darlin', and even if you don't want to tell me about it now, I'll find out sooner or later." He chuckled gleefully, then repeated, "I'll find out. You just wait and see."

"Eb, you're getting senile!" She laughed, hiding her wariness. "If I look different it's because I'm anticipating a whole month away from my two wrinkle makers."

"How many times've you tried to fool me, Abby?" He cackled loudly at her disgruntled expression. "And how many times have you actually pulled it off?"

Before she could deny his charge, they heard a shout from the two-story house that Eb had called home for more than sixty years.

"That feebleminded old busybody," he grumbled. "It must be time for my medicine. I swear she sits around watching the clock just so she can holler at me when it's time for me to take one of those blasted horse pills Harding gives me."

"What did she say?" Abby whispered, leaning closer as she shook her head in bewilderment. She had known Eb's housekeeper, Mrs. Rappaport, for twenty years and had never been able to understand what she was saying. It was not that she had an accent, but she always mumbled and talked around in circles without ever really touching on the subject under discussion. "I didn't hear anything about medicine."

"Aw, she's spouting Proverbs again. 'A slothful man hideth his hand in his bosom,'" he mimicked. "Now what the hell's that supposed to mean? If I'm gonna be feeling around on somebody's bosom, it's damn sure not gonna be my own."

He ignored Abby's shout of surprised laughter, his eyes narrowing as he looked over his shoulder at his house. Then a devilish guffaw escaped him. "I think I'll go pinch her bony behind. That ought to get me the whole book of Job . . . with a little Deuteronomy thrown in for good measure."

"You're a dirty old man, Eb Watson!" Abby called after him as he made his way across the yard, but the only answer she got was a snort of gleeful laughter.

An hour later, as Abby dodged holes in the dirt road that led to her parents' farm, she was still thinking of the change Eb had said he could see in her. Was it really the thought of having time to herself? Or was it, as she suspected, the memory of Joe he had seen "bubbling up" in her eyes? She had to admit she felt different. But could one small encounter with a man make that much difference? she wondered.

One small encounter? That somehow didn't seem an adequate description for what had happened to her that night beside the lake. She had come away from it feeling totally different about herself as a woman. Suddenly it wasn't enough to be the Widow Fisher, schoolteacher, and mother to Jeff and Brennie. Suddenly she had felt as though there might be more to this person, Abigail Fisher, than she had ever suspected.

As her parents' home appeared around the next corner, she shook away the thought, telling herself she was getting a little too fanciful for her own good. Abby was not one to dwell on fairy tales; it was practical reality that counted with her. And dreams of a prince who would kiss her awake—dreams of Joe—were simply not practical.

She pulled the station wagon into the gravel driveway and, as she stepped from the car, she slipped back into the comfortable, familiar role of much-loved and still-indulged only daughter. Although her parents had accepted her as an adult the moment she'd married Don, they had never let her forget that they were there for her when and if she needed them.

It was only as she was leaving several hours later that Abby's own daughter brought the puzzle of her relationship with Joe back into her thoughts.

"Are you sure you'll be all right?" Brennie stared down at her mother through the open car window.

Abby looked into the worried eyes, so very much like her own, and smiled reassuringly. "I'll call once a week, Brennie. And I promise I'll be fine."

"But you've never been on your own for a whole month before. What will you do?"

"For a start, I'll sit and listen to the quiet." She paused thoughtfully. "Then maybe I'll just hang around and watch the house stay clean."

Abby certainly couldn't tell her that she didn't anticipate being alone. She didn't know for sure that she would see Joe again and, even if she had known, how could she tell Brennie that she was looking forward to being pursued by an ex-quarterback?

"Come on, Bren," Abby coaxed. "Jeff's not worried about me. Why should you be?"

"Jeff's a nerd and a cretin."

"Cretin?" Abby looked impressed. "Is that this week's word?" At her daughter's grin and nod, she added, "Well, I suppose it's better than mutant."

She started to say something more to reassure her daughter that she would not be lonely, but already Brennie's thoughts were turning to her grandparents and the pig that had been designated hers for their stay.

I'm forgotten already, she thought with a rueful smile. But Abby didn't really mind. She knew it was healthy. Her children would be very well occupied for the next month.

But would she? Abby wondered. Brennie was right. This was the first time in her life that she had been truly alone for more than a few days at a time. She was determined to make the most of her vacation, but she felt a little lost. Suddenly she was nothing more than Abigail Fisher. Not mother, not daughter, only woman.

Woman. Somehow over the last few years she had forgotten that before all her other roles she was a woman. It was strange that only now did the fact stand out. Was it Joe who had brought it home to her?

"I'm a woman. He's a man," she said, testing the words aloud. It sounded very simple on the surface, but Abby knew it wasn't. Joe had roles too. And his didn't stop at just being a man, even though he was very much a man.

So much a man, she thought wryly, that each time she picked up a gossip newspaper she saw a picture of him with a different woman. And it seemed that he had never tried to discourage the rumors about his private life. In fact, there were times, on the late-night talk shows and in scandal sheet interviews, when he seemed to be going out of his way to provide additional fuel for the gossips.

Women were his life's work, according to the media. That was the impression he gave, and considering the way he made her feel, it wasn't hard to believe. But there was that secret smile, as though he were playing a great joke on life.

But then there was the way he had been with the boys over the weekend, she mused. Hardly the behavior of a playboy. She grinned. With Joe's sense of humor, he was probably putting the whole world on. And enjoying every minute of it.

But playboy or practical joker, he was still the most exciting man she had ever met, Abby thought with a smile as she turned her full concentration to the road ahead of her.

When she walked into the house an hour later, she stood for a moment listening. So this was what silence sounded like, she thought, raising her brows in wonder.

Feeling a nudge against her leg, she glanced down. "Look at me, Merry," she said to the puppy. "Really look at me. Am I Brennie and Jeff's mother? Or Don's widow? Or Sally and John's daughter?" Giving a sleepy woof, the dog moved away to curl up on his cushion in the corner of the room, ignoring her wistful questions.

She inhaled deeply. As much as she loved her children, she felt free, really free, for the first time in years. She could do anything she wanted to do without having to worry about Brennie and Jeff. The problem was what to do. She had never had unlimited time before. There had always been soccer games and piano recitals and all the daily emergencies that made life as a mother so exciting.

Suddenly, as it occurred to her that she could even do absolutely nothing without feeling guilty about wasting time, she began to laugh light-headedly. Then she turned toward the door at the sound of the doorbell.

As she opened it, her eyes widened in surprise. Joe stood on the porch, holding the screen door open, and his eyes were trained on something above her head. Her gaze slid stealthily over his tight brown slacks and tan sport jacket, then quickly followed his upward.

"Your weather stripping is loose," he said, and

lowered his eyes to her, his mouth forming a smile that would have melted the middle of an Oreo cookie at ten paces.

She stared at him quizzically for a moment, tiny lines of concentration appearing between her arched brows. Then her lips formed an O of comprehension. "Just a minute—I think I have one," she said quickly. "How about—Your mother wears combat boots?"

He laughed softly as he moved to lean against the doorjamb, bringing his face closer to hers.

Oh, help, she thought frantically. How could she have forgotten that this was the man who turned her knees to pistachio pudding with just a look?

Swallowing loudly, she took a small step backward and murmured cautiously, "You didn't stop by just to trade insults with me, did you?"

"No."

He stepped into the room and closed the door behind him. The sound echoed loudly in the empty house. This was something she hadn't thought about. Always before when they'd met, they had been surrounded by people. She hadn't realized how much that had affected his behavior. And her reaction to him.

"I heard that Jeff and Brennie were staying with your parents and I just wanted to make sure you weren't . . ." he paused and the smile widened, ". . . lonely."

His words were oh, so casual, but the look in his eyes was anything but, Abby thought. Again she slowly backed away, changing directions abruptly when she bumped into the lamp table beside the brown leather recliner.

"Lonely?" She gave a breathless laugh. "I've been looking forward to this vacation for ages." She raised her hand to brush the hair from her forehead in a nervous gesture and kept walking unsteadily backwards. "I've got a three-page list of 'Things To Do While The Kids Are Gone.'" Every backward step she took was matched by an equal step forward from Joe.

"Such as?" he pressed.

How could two words sound so provocative . . . so suggestive? she wondered in harried bewilderment. She tried the laugh again but it was no less breathless than the first time. "I've got a dozen best-sellers that I've saved to read while they're gone and—and other things like . . ." She searched for something, anything, to say.

"Like?" He moved a step closer.

"The weather stripping!" she said in a relieved gust. "I need to—oh!" Abby stopped speaking abruptly as her back connected with the wall.

Raising one hand to the wall beside her, Joe leaned closer; then his other hand came up to rest somewhere next to her waist, trapping her between the solid wall and his even more solid body.

"You need to . . . what?" he murmured, stirring the fine hair on her forehead.

Swallowing the lump in her throat, she gasped, "Replace it." She moistened her lips, then clamped them down over her tongue when she saw his eyes following the movement. "Yes, I definitely"—she stifled a groan that began forming deep within her as he eased the lower part of his body against hers—"need to replace it."

"I've heard"—he leaned even closer and she felt

loved being around all that enthusiasm. Most adults lose it somewhere along the way, and high school kids don't have it yet . . . they just want to get out of school. But when they enter college, it's as if they suddenly discover that the world is out there waiting for them to put a dent in it." Her lips turned up in a wistful smile. "Of course, when they get older they realize the world doesn't dent so easily. And that's a shame, because it's the ones who really believe they can make a change who eventually do."

Joe leaned forward in his cross-legged position and pulled at a blade of grass, his brow wrinkled in thought. "I know what you mean. Some people manage to do the impossible simply because someone forgot to tell them it was impossible."

"Exactly." She clasped her arms around her knees. "But as far as finding myself there, I just don't know. Do you suppose anyone ever realizes it when it happens?"

"Maybe the problem is that no one ever really finds himself," he said quietly. Lying back and resting his head on his hands, he stared up at the stars. "We're all constantly changing, constantly growing, so the me of today isn't necessarily the me of tomorrow."

Abby sprawled beside him and gave a small laugh. "I think this is getting a little deep for me, but before I change the subject to something trivial, I'll add just one more thought from the all-encompassing store of knowledge held by Abigail Fisher. I think there are some people who could find themselves if they wanted to look, but they're afraid of what they might find, so they don't bother. Those are the ones who don't grow. They the warmth of his breath against her ear—"that replacing weather stripping can be hard work." A shiver of desire ran down her body, visibly shaking her as he sucked her earlobe gently, giving it a tiny nip before continuing. "Maybe we should go out to eat first, so you'll have enough energy for . . ." he paused, and the hand that had been beside her waist was now on her hip, pressing her closer to his blatantly aroused masculinity, ". . . weather stripping."

"Actually," she gasped, her eyelids slowly closing as she felt his hips move against hers, "I hadn't planned on leaving the house tonight."

"That might work out better," he said, lowering his head the fraction of an inch it took to find her lips. He brought his hand up between them to capture her breast and she shivered, feeling as though she had been waiting forever for his touch, his kiss.

Keep cool and calm. Fight the feeling, her brain urged bracingly.

Mind your own business, her body countered as it moved deeper into his embrace.

It was only when she felt his fingers on the buttons of her blouse that a measure of sanity returned. It was happening too fast. She was losing control more quickly than she had ever dreamed. She had to remember the game. She had to remember her position in her hometown.

Oh Lord, she moaned silently. Was this the end of the game? There was no way she could give in to him, but how on earth was she going to make her reluctant body leave the incredibly erotic sweetness of his arms?

She looked frantically around the room for an

avenue of escape. Then her eyes came to rest on the cushion in the corner of the room.

"Joe—listen," she gasped. "You've got to stop."

Somehow her weak words didn't seem to convince him, for he didn't stop. Instead his lips moved to the top of one rounded breast and she heard him utter a breathless laugh when a moan of pleasure escaped her.

"Joe," she repeated, "all I have to do is say the word and Merry will attack you."

"Merry?" He raised his head briefly, but only to laugh again softly.

"Merry, get him!" The words weren't as firm as she had planned, but Merry heard and came bounding across the room. She heaved a sigh of relief. Then, as she stared down at her rescuer, her eyes lifted to heaven in resigned dismay.

Joe turned sideways, resting his elbow against the wall. Then he stared down at Merry as the puppy stubbornly held on to the hem of Abby's slacks with his teeth, vigorously shaking his head back and forth.

"He's fearsome, all right," he said, grinning broadly. Then he told the puppy firmly, "Dog! That's enough."

Sighing in resignation, Abby watched as the loyal animal reacted immediately to the command. "Traitor," she muttered.

Joe smiled and leaned close again. "Now let's get back to where we were . . . unless you can think of another tactic to delay me."

He sounded too confident. And why shouldn't he be? she thought. Between her traitorous body and equally traitorous dog, it looked as if he had won the game even before it had begun.

"Well?" he prompted.

"I can think of a few," she murmured, "but somehow the Lord never sends floods or earthquakes when you really need them."

He chuckled deep in his throat and the effect of the sound on her senses made her doubt that even the advent of those disasters would break the hold he had on her.

"Do you really want me to stop?" he asked. "Why don't you admit how you feel when I touch you?"

Her heart began to pound in her chest at the softly spoken words, but she lifted her chin firmly. "You want me to forfeit the game? I'm not so poor-spirited."

Her statement seemed to stop him for a moment; then he moved and his lips were only a whisper away. "Forget the game, Abby. Tell me how you feel when I do this." Gently lifting her breast in the palm of his hand, he moved his callused thumb back and forth across one lace-covered nipple, watching in fascination as it sprang out taut. "And when I do this." His other hand slid down her ribs across her stomach to rest on the warmth between her thighs.

The earthquake she had wished for suddenly shook her, rising from the fiery epicenter where his hand lay and radiating forcefully through her body, weakening her limbs. And she wasn't alone on that shaking spot of earth. She could feel Joe's heart racing in his chest where it pressed against her.

The sighing moan that accompanied the weakness had barely left her lips when she heard a knock on her front door. The sound effectively accomplished what she hadn't been able to do alone, and only Joe's strong arms kept her from sliding bonelessly down the wall to the floor as the tension seeped out of her body.

She opened dazed eyes and stared at him, her lips curving in an unsteady smile. "It seems," she whispered breathlessly, "that we underestimated each other." Drawing a shaky breath, she pulled away to straighten her clothes. "You almost had me that time," she admitted slowly.

His eyes remained closed for a moment and he seemed to be willing his heart to slow its hectic pace. Then he opened his eyes lazily and grinned as he looked down at her. "You think *that* was something? Give me thirty minutes without interruptions and you won't know what hit you."

She laughed. She couldn't help it. Never had she heard such braggadocio, such swollen-headed gall. "I don't think you need me at all," she said, shaking her head. "You're already having a marvelous love affair with yourself."

A more determined knock on the door forced her to shelve the other comments she wanted to make. She turned and walked quickly across the room, smoothing her hair to the sound of his delighted laughter.

"Judy," she said warily, opening the door a couple of inches and placing her body in the opening to block her friend's view of the room. All she needed now was a confrontation with this adorable busybody.

But her hesitation went unnoticed by Harrison's energetic wife. Abby felt the doorknob connect with her belly button before she prudently stepped out of the way. The blond locomotive pushed her way in.

"Abby, I just wanted to tell you—oh, *hello*, Joe." She turned to give Abby a sly look. "How nice to see you here," Judy said with the smug satisfaction of one who told-you-so. "I just knew you two would hit it off once we got you together."

Abby shot Joe a look of exasperated apology. "Judy, what did you want to tell me?"

Her friend's eyes brightened as she remembered. "This is perfect! I wanted to ask you to come to our barbecue tonight—it's a last-minute thing. Harrison decided to charcoal steaks and you know him. He wasn't satisfied until he had asked everyone in the county to join us." She glanced at Joe, then at Abby. "Now you can both come. Everyone—"

"We can't! We're going—"

"We have reservations—"

Joe and Abby spoke simultaneously with great haste, then stopped abruptly. Joe's eyes crinkled with triumphant humor and Abby tried very hard to be annoyed, but failed miserably.

"It's thoughtful of you to ask," Joe said, "but we have plans we just can't get out of."

"That's a shame," Judy said in disappointment; then her eyes brightened as she added, "As long as I'm here I can talk to Joe while you get dressed, Abby. Have I told you that Abby started teaching Sunday school when she was only fourteen? Everyone—"

Judy's reminiscence was cut off sharply when Abby jerked her in the direction of the bedroom. "Help me dress, Judy," Abby said grimly, giving Joe a dark, squelching look that affected his amusement not one whit.

"Really, Abby," Judy protested as the bedroom door closed behind them, "you've been dressing yourself for years. Why do you suddenly need my help?"

"I don't. But I also don't need you to sell me to Joe." She walked to the closet and opened it, then gave her clothes a disgusted look.

"I wasn't trying to sell you. But Joe's special. He—"

"Yes, I know," Abby interrupted, grinning over her shoulder. "He makes shaving cream commercials."

"I was going to say he's gorgeous." She joined Abby by the open closet door. "You're too casual about this," Judy murmured distractedly as she flipped through the clothes. "You know, you really are going to have to buy some decent clothes. I don't see a single thing that—" She broke off as Abby pulled a sky blue silk sheath from the closet.

"What do you think?" Abby asked, holding it against her.

"I remember this." Judy reached out to touch the silk. "You wore it to that banquet just before Don died. It looked great on you, and the style's still good."

"I've gained weight since then. I hope it still fits." Stripping quickly she pulled on the blue silk sheath, then turned around to let her friend zip it up. When she turned around, Judy's face went strangely still.

"Oh, my," she said with quiet emphasis, "it didn't look like that when you wore it to the banquet."

Abby walked to the mirror and stared for a moment at the deep V neck that exposed a good portion of her full breasts. "I told you I've gained weight."

After what had just happened in the living room, Abby felt she should be changing into something with long sleeves and a high neck . . . perhaps in mud brown. Then a determined light began to grow in her eyes. She wouldn't be so cowardly, she decided. She would play the game with panache, throwing him as many curves as he threw her.

She turned to find Judy staring at her with a wicked look in her eyes. After a moment the blonde smiled and murmured slowly, "It couldn't hurt."

Abby burst out laughing, shaking her head as she said, "I don't believe it."

"There's no need to look shocked, Abby. I know something about attracting the opposite sex. How do you think I landed Harrison . . . and kept him hopping all these years?"

The thought of plump, homey Judy showing indiscreet amounts of flesh in order to capture Harrison was too much for Abby's imagination and her laughter grew.

It took a while for her to calm down enough to put on makeup and give her hair a good brushing, but twenty minutes later she was ready. Before leaving the bedroom, Abby threw a black shawl around her shoulders, then accompanied her friend to the front door.

It took another five minutes for Judy to say good-bye to Joe, but finally Abby closed the door behind her meddlesome but thoroughly delightful friend. Then she turned to confront the dark eyes that had been burning into her since she had reentered the living room.

Five

Joe watched Abby complete her slow turn. He had to hide a grin when her eyes widened upon finding he had advanced quietly and was now standing only a few feet away from her.

He remained silent as his warm gaze slid over her silk-clad body. Her golden brown hair was pulled back on each side and held with gold clasps. The blue dress hugged her hips and thighs provocatively, making him wonder what was beneath the shawl she clutched so tightly at her breasts. "Hel-*lo*, beautiful schoolteacher," he breathed softly.

She swallowed and began circling him warily as he moved closer. "Hel-*lo*, thickheaded quarterback," she said hesitantly. Then she sidestepped quickly and began to walk away.

Without taking a step he grasped her arm and pulled her back against him. "Going somewhere?" he asked close to her ear, trying to keep the laughter out of his voice.

"Me?" she scoffed weakly. "Of course not. We're going out . . . remember?"

72

He loosened his grip a little and looked down at her in surprise. "You're really going out with me?"

As though taking him by surprise had restored her confidence, he felt the muscles in her arms gradually relax. "I've explained all this to you," she said, a gleam of amusement beginning to grow in her gray-green eyes. "How many people do you think will be watching when we walk out that door? I've already told Judy I'm going out with you."

She glanced down at her watch. "She's been gone about two minutes so she's had enough time to inform all of Bardle and half of New Jersey by now. If I don't leave with you, they'll be over here en masse to find out why."

With comic haste, Joe dropped her arm and glanced nervously over his shoulder. He suddenly felt as though all her friends were peeking in at them. Running a finger around the collar of his shirt, he glanced back at Abby. "You're kidding, right?"

She laughed as his eyes looked toward the window again. "Ready to call it quits, sport?"

Suddenly his discomfort disappeared. She was enjoying this little scene entirely too much, he decided. Moving swiftly, he placed a hand on the doorjamb above her head and leaned closer. "Do you really think I give up that easily?"

His free hand played with the soft fabric of the shawl draped around her shoulders. Then, with a gentle tug, he removed it from her grasping fingers. As his eyes settled on the golden, rounded flesh framed by blue silk, he inhaled quickly.

After a tense moment he felt composed enough to give a short, rough laugh. "You did it on purpose, didn't you?" He shook his head ruefully, wondering if she could see his heart banging against his chest. "When will I learn not to underestimate you? You tell me the whole county is watching, then . . ." He paused, drawing a finger down the bare flesh between her breasts.

She gave him a wide-eyed, nonchalant "who me?" stare, but Joe knew she wasn't feeling as complacent as she looked. The skin under his fingertip trembled perceptibly at his touch. She seemed to be struggling to organize her thoughts. After a moment she glanced up at him through her long lashes and said, "You're not going to chase me around the room again, are you?"

He inhaled slowly, then scooped her close in an exuberant bear hug. "Abigail Fisher, you'll either be the death or the making of me," he said, laughing in delight. "And if it's death . . . what a way to go," he added as he ushered her out the front door.

He drove with purpose and didn't slow down as he passed the Dairy Queen, Bodacious Barbeque, and All-you-can-eat for $5.99 Catfish Cabin— the only restaurants in Bardle. Then he turned onto Route 75 into Dallas.

"Are you taking me to one of your Shrimp Shacks?" she asked, resting her arm on the seat as she turned sideways to look at him inquiringly.

He smiled. "No, not unless your heart is set on it. Do you remember when I told you there were things that I wanted to teach you?" She nodded, raising one arched brow. "Yes, I know what you thought," he continued, "but tonight I'm going to teach you how to have fun."

"You make me sound very dull," she said. "I know how to have fun."

"I'm not talking about secondhand fun—through your kids or your students or your neighbors. I'm going to teach you to have fun for Abby's sake." Before she could voice a protest, he continued. "As nice as it is, you happen to live in a very limiting environment. In Bardle you're seen as a teacher, a widow, and a mother. You live up to the restrictions other people put on you."

She shook her head slowly. "You certainly have formed some strong opinions in the short time you've been here. And I'm afraid they're not entirely correct. My friends don't limit me. They all want only the best for me."

"Yes, you're right," he admitted. "But it's the best as they see it. And you've got to realize they've known you so long, you're locked into a role that's taken a lifetime to develop. If you decided to live a different lifestyle, they would accept it because they love you. It's *you* who would have trouble breaking the mold, not them."

Catching her quick glance, he laughed suddenly. "You think I'm a little too pompous, a little too sure of my opinions, don't you? It doesn't matter. Just give me a chance." He picked up her hand and urged her to slide closer to him. "You know how you take your car in for an engine tune-up? Tonight *you're* going in for a tune-up. You're long overdue for an attitude adjustment. I'm going to show you a different world, one where obligations don't exist. Fun is the password."

Abby didn't comment. He was right about one thing—she thought he was a little too sure of his opinions. He'd come into the game too late to know that much about her life. But it didn't matter. She was perfectly willing to let him lead tonight. It wouldn't hurt to try his new world for a while. She knew it wouldn't work when Jeff and Brennie came home and when school began again. But for right now, why not? she thought.

On Greenville Avenue he pulled into the crowded parking lot of a small place that Abby had only read about in the "People" section of the Sunday papers. The owners had wanted to create something along the lines of a New York supper club and apparently they had succeeded, for the small club was quickly gaining a reputation as the "in" place to go.

It was a place out of a dream, Abby thought. White on white on white, with elegant touches of gold in the cluster of candlesticks that decorated each linen-covered table and in the almost unseen flecks in the plush white carpet. It was an F. Scott Fitzgerald kind of place and it took Abby's breath away. It was several minutes before she managed to adjust to the way the club made her feel— ultrafeminine and very special.

In the flickering candlelight Abby studied Joe intently while he gave their orders to the waiter. His harsh good looks didn't seem at all out of place. In fact, it seemed as though the surroundings had in some way adjusted to him, instead of the other way around. It made her wonder again about his background.

When he'd handed back the menus, she asked, "How long have you known Harrison?" Before he could answer, she added, "You said you owed him. I don't remember your ever having been in Bardle before so I thought maybe it was an old debt."

He nodded thoughtfully. "An old debt," he

repeated. "Yes, it certainly is that. I met Harrison in Brooklyn."

"Brooklyn?" she echoed in surprise. "But Harrison left Brooklyn right after high school, didn't he?"

He nodded. "Twenty-two years ago. We were both born and raised in Brooklyn."

That surprised her. Not about Harrison; she knew his background, but about Joe. He didn't have the slightest trace of a Brooklyn accent.

"Did you know his father was a high school coach?" he asked before she could comment.

She shook her head. "I'm really closer to Judy than to Harrison. He's a friend, but not a confidant." She paused, then asked hesitantly, "Does Harrison's father have something to do with the debt you owe him?"

He nodded slowly, fingering his wineglass, then smiled a crooked, slightly sad smile. "I guess you could say I had problems when I was younger."

"What kind—" she began, then shook her head sharply. "No, I'm sorry. That's none of my business."

"No." He covered her hand. "I want to tell you. It's funny, you know. I always get a warm feeling when I think of Harrison, but it's been a long time since I actually thought about why. I had a giant hate going back then, Abby. A hate that I thought included the whole world, centering most intensely on my parents. But I found out later"—he laughed mirthlessly—"much later, that I didn't hate anyone."

She turned her hand and squeezed his fingers. "I'd like to hear, if you don't mind talking about it."

He gave her a warm smile. "I don't mind talking to you about anything. When I was six my mother left. Just walked out without a word. My father . . . my father was not a loving person," he said ruefully. "What the hell—there's no nice way to say it. He abused me."

She sucked in a sharp, shocked breath. He'd said it so bluntly, as though he were talking about nothing more important than the day's news.

When he heard her indrawn breath, he shook his head and smiled. "Don't let it upset you. It was a long time ago. Actually, it was only occasionally physical abuse; more often it was mental. There were times when I really believed he hated me. Over the years I've come to realize that it was himself he hated most of all. I guess he thought he saw all his bad qualities in me. That's what I tell myself now, but even rationalizing doesn't entirely stop it from hurting. The very sight of me made him explosively angry. He seemed to feel—oh, I don't know—some kind of deep need to knock me down. He would tell me over and over how worthless I was."

He spread his hands in a gesture of futility. "I could never understand what I had done. For a long time I was sure it was my fault my mother had left. I felt guilty about all my childhood sins. Being too loud. Getting my new shoes muddy. I figured that was why he hated me."

Abby felt a painful fury well up inside her and had to bite her lip to keep the angry words inside. She thought of her ebullient Jeff and tried to imagine his inner joy squelched by such hurt. Taking a deep, calming breath, she stared at the piano in the corner of the room and blinked away tears that stung. She listened as he went on.

"Some people react to that kind of situation by crawling into a protective shell. But not me." She heard the grin in his voice and turned back to find that the sun had come out again for her. "I was the biggest hell-raiser you've ever seen. There wasn't a teacher in grade school who could handle me. By the time I was eleven I had already been in reform school for habitual truancy."

She gasped. "Can they do that? I thought you had to commit a crime or something."

"Not if your parents agree to it, and my father agreed. It's probably a good thing it happened." He grinned suddenly. "I may have been wild, but I wasn't stupid. It was . . . it was not a nice place, so after that I went to school every day—religiously. Of course, I saw to it that the teachers knew I didn't want to be there."

She smiled at the wicked gleam in his eyes, concentrating fiercely on his words because she didn't want to think about the strange feeling that was overtaking her. The feeling that nothing in her life would ever be the same again. The feeling that Joe was reaching inside her to touch a part that had never been touched before.

"I met Harrison in high school," he went on. "Lord, I was a pain in the ass back then, so contemptuous of the fact that his father was the football coach. I thought those pampered all-American jocks at school were a bunch of sissies." He smiled ruefully. "I admit now that I was jealous. Jealous of the normalcy of their lives. But back then I thought I was cool. For some crazy reason Harrison decided he wanted to be my friend." He shook his head and smiled ruefully. "I gave him hell. I made fun of him, told him over and over again to get lost, and did anything I could to humiliate him." He shrugged. "But nothing stopped him. He kept coming back. He was the one who convinced me to try out for the team . . . and convinced his father to give me a chance. I told myself I was doing it just to show those mama's boys how a real man plays football, but secretly I wanted so badly to be a part of that world."

He laughed softly. "The first time I went out on the field those 'mama's boys' creamed me. And that made me all the more determined to prove myself." He smiled. "So, that's how it all started. Later there was a football scholarship. And even later came the realization that I had never hated anyone . . . except maybe myself." His brows drew together as if his head ached. "That was painful. I found out that, like every other human being, I just wanted to be accepted for what I was."

He looked startled for a moment, as though he had come back to the present with a jolt. "Damn," he said with quiet emphasis. "I haven't talked about that in years. And here I was wanting to impress you with what a suave character I am."

She smiled slightly. "I'm impressed," she said slowly. "Take my word for it."

Suddenly the waiter appeared beside them with their first course and the serious mood that had held them both disappeared. They ate in companionable silence, listening to the veteran singer who performed with only a piano for accompaniment. It didn't take Abby long to realize this wasn't a run-of-the-mill show; the stout singer didn't sing "Feelings" even once, but went through a long list of Cole Porter songs. She sang some of his hits, but many more of the lesser known pieces, including some that had been cut from Broadway musicals.

"She's wonderful," Abby said, leaning across the table so Joe could hear her over the piano. The singer had paused momentarily to take a drink of water from one of the waiters.

"She's the reason I chose this place. I heard her in New York, only there she was doing Irving Berlin."

"You like Irving Berlin?" Abby could hear it in his voice.

"Love him," he said emphatically. "He was strictly American, even though he was born in Russia." At her inquisitive look his lips twisted in a smile that was almost shy. "All right, I admit it. I love America and anything American. I know that makes me something of an oddity."

"Oddity?" she said with raised brows. "Nowadays that makes you a rebel."

"It's worse than you think," he admitted with a grin. "Every time I hear the part in 'The Star Spangled Banner' where he finds that the flag has survived the bombs, I get choked up."

She opened her mouth to tease him, but found she couldn't. She admired him too much for what he had admitted. "I do too," she confessed. " 'This Land Is My Land' and 'God Bless America' make me tear up every time. Show me blatant, old-fashioned, corny patriotism and I cry like a baby," she finished with heartfelt enthusiasm. What had started as a hesitant confession had become a proud statement of fact that for no reason set them laughing.

It felt good to laugh with him, Abby thought. It felt good to have her hand in his as they listened to the rest of the show. In fact, being with Joe made her feel happier than she had in so long.

After they left the supper club, Joe took her to one of the small clubs that line Greenville Avenue. They walked through the door and into a world unknown to Abby. For a few minutes she was lost amid the music and loud voices and smoke, but before she could catch her breath, Joe had her out on the dance floor, where she felt breathless changes taking place inside her. It was as though some part of her that had been overlooked for years was beginning to struggle for freedom.

As she circled Joe once again on the crowded dance floor, she called out, "Joe, am I boogying?"

He threw back his head and laughed, causing more than one pair of female eyes to gleam with interest. "You're definitely boogying, Abby," he confirmed.

She nodded in satisfaction, then turned to smile at a tall teenager to her left.

She and Joe danced without pause for the next two hours, stopping only when Abby felt that her legs had taken on a life of their own and were threatening mutiny. Then they quickly traded the noisy club for a small nearby pub with a distinctly Irish flavor.

An ongoing game of darts held everyone's attention and after a while Abby let Joe persuade her to try her hand, even though some of the spectators felt it wasn't in keeping with the spirit of the game when Abby insisted on sitting down to throw the small, heavy missiles.

After the game—which Joe won only because her darts seemed to have an unnatural fascination for the plaster wall surrounding the dart board—

she lost all sense of time. She sat beside Joe and talked with the pub regulars about Ireland and horse racing and jazz.

It was an exhilarating experience for Abby. She was used to conversing either with children or adults who, though wonderful people, didn't think about much beyond the town boundaries of Bardle.

When they left the pub at last, it was two in the morning. Abby felt relaxed and happy but in no way tired. As she sat close to Joe in the car, softly singing "Sweet Molly Malone," she felt she could stay up forever.

He joined her for the last "alive, alive-o," then glanced down at her and smiled. "I don't want to go home," he said wistfully.

She gave a husky laugh. "Neither do I, but I wasn't going to mention it."

At that moment they passed a small, beautifully landscaped park, the vapor lights spotlighting a dozen pieces of playground equipment for the neighborhood children. They looked at each other, then grinned simultaneously as he swung the car around in a quick U-turn.

Five minutes later she was stretching her toes to the stars in an attempt to outswing him. "I'll beat you, quarterback," she called out.

He laughed. "You're always throwing out challenges," he called back. "Consciously and unconsciously. You'd better learn now that I don't pass up either kind."

"What kind of unconscious challenges have I been throwing out?" she asked, letting her swing slow to a gentle rock.

"You said I couldn't seduce you," he said as his swing slowed to match her pace.

"That wasn't a challenge; that was a fact." She wrapped her arms around the chains that held the wooden swing and clasped her hands together. "I didn't say you couldn't make love to me. I merely said that if you did, it would be my choice." She ignored the way her heart began to pound as his eyes took on an intimate, sensual look, and she added quickly, "That was only one instance . . . and a poor one at that. What other challenges?"

"Your whole lifestyle is a challenge. You've let me see the mother Abby and the teacher Abby and even the friend Abby, but you've only let me see glimpses of the woman Abby." He paused as she shifted uncomfortably. "It makes me wonder if you even know that that Abby exists. Who are you, Abby, when there's no one around to tell you which role you should be playing?"

Who was she? she thought. She didn't like the question. It made her feel insecure suddenly, and she wasn't used to insecurity. It was doubly hard to take since it came only a few hours after she herself had been questioning her identity.

"Forget it," he ordered softly, smiling into her eyes. "Forget I mentioned that. I'll find out for myself . . . and maybe I'll find out for you."

He jumped abruptly from the swing and grabbed her hand. "Come seesaw with me. I didn't get much chance to do this kind of thing when I was a kid and I plan to correct that deficiency tonight."

"Seesaw! You've got to be kidding; you must weigh seventy-five pounds more than I do."

"Didn't you ever learn about the fulcrum? If

you sit way back on the end and I sit up close"—he showed her—"like this, it'll work just fine."

"Sure it will," she said, nodding her head. "And who do you suppose will pick me up when I shoot over your head and land in Detroit?"

But happily she found that Archimedes' Law still worked, and so they seesawed, a little shakily because of her sidesaddle position, but with enthusiasm. And they slid, a dozen times down the wide triple wave slide that was built into the side of a hill. And they whirled on the merry-go-round until they were both dizzy and weak with laughter.

Joe didn't want it to stop. He almost ached as he studied her laughing face. There was something there that pulled at him, something for which he must have been looking for years without knowing it.

He tried to tell himself that it was because she was part of the "normal" world that he still yearned to join, only somehow it didn't ring true. That might have been a small part of the attraction, he acknowledged, but the major part was simply that she was Abby. Indefinable, beckoning, enthralling Abby.

From the moment he'd met her she had begun weaving a fine web around his heart—a silken web, a web of steel—forged by his own needs. She smiled and the web became more secure. She touched him and it tightened immeasurably.

Somehow he had to find the woman in her, had to make her see that the game was over and a relationship was beginning. But Joe knew already that it wouldn't be an easy process. At this moment she was feeling a great satisfaction in simply having a good time, the fun he had promised her, but he could tell she considered it merely a temporary escape. She seemed to be keeping this part, the woman part, separate from what she considered reality, he decided. She was not ready to let him into the mainstream of her life. Not yet, he added silently.

"So what did you think of my world?" he asked as he pulled up in front of her house. The street was dark and quiet.

She leaned her head back against the seat, turning slightly to look at him. "It was wonderful . . . a little like Disneyland for grown-ups."

"Disneyland," he echoed thoughtfully. "As in fantasy or something not quite real?"

"You have to admit that it's just a place to visit. It's exactly what I needed for my first vacation alone and I thank you. But . . ."

"But?"

She smiled and the smile held elements he couldn't define. "But when the kids come home, my life will return to normal and it will all be a very pleasant memory."

Joe winced inside. *He* was included in the things that would be relegated to memory. She didn't say it, perhaps didn't even consciously recognize it herself. But he knew it as certainly as he knew he wasn't going to settle for a vague spot in the back of her mind without a fight.

Abby stared at him silently, wondering what was going through his mind, wondering what was causing the strange expression on his face.

He turned to find her watching him and moved slightly to kiss her forehead. Then, as though he found the discreet show of affection as inadequate as she did, his arms tightened around her and he bent to meet her waiting lips.

She eagerly lifted her hands to his face, wanting to hold the kiss forever. She liked the solid feel of his jaw, the hard feel of his flesh. Strong and masculine, it echoed his personality. Her touch brought an electricity to the air around them and he let his head fall to her breasts.

Suddenly he gave a rough, breathless laugh. "And I was going to seduce you?" he whispered huskily. "You seduce me with every touch."

Abby placed her hands on either side of his head and pressed him closer, moving her breasts against him slowly. She lowered her hands and released a button on his shirt, in order to slide her hand inside next to his skin.

His groan of pleasure shook her visibly and she whispered through dry, hot lips, "I was right about not being seduced . . . because I know exactly what I'm doing . . . and why I'm doing it. I'm doing it because I want to. Because I can't *not* touch you."

He made a sound that was painful to hear and his lips met hers in a fiery kiss. In the next few minutes a delicious heat surrounded them in waves as their bodies moved desperately against each other. His fingers found the zipper at the back of her dress and the fabric parted with a sensual whisper. She wasn't as quick with the other buttons on his shirt, but finally their upper bodies were melded together, flesh to flesh, two feverish sighs of pleasure meeting and merging.

"Joe," she said, the word taking the form of a gasp for breath. "Oh Lord, Joe. This is too much. Too much, too fast. I'm in over my head." She held on to him and whispered urgently against his jaw, his throat, "I really, really am."

Taking her face in his hands, he held her an inch away and stared into her eyes. "You really, really are?" he repeated huskily. After a moment his lips twisted in a wry smile. "Yes, I guess you are."

He brought her head to rest on his shoulder and they sat there for long moments as their breathing returned to normal. "How about a cup of coffee instead?" he said finally. "I know it's only postponing the inevitable, but I don't want to leave just yet."

At her nod of agreement, they adjusted their clothes and he slid out of the car, silently bending down to help her out. Words didn't seem to be necessary now. She knew he would kiss her again, but she also knew he wouldn't press for more. It was as though the end of the evening had been planned between them down to its most minute detail.

She stepped from the car into the warm, seductive night air. But as she reached the sidewalk, the unspoken plan went sadly awry. An unseen demon entered her legs, causing her knees to buckle slightly.

She lurched sideways just enough to collide with Billy Don Bosier's wagon. Four-year-old Billy Don was the terror of the neighborhood, and his wagon contained the tools of his trade, an assortment of battered pots and pans in which to carry sand and bugs and to beat on when the street became too peaceful.

Suddenly the whole street came alive. Mere seconds after the quiet had been broken by the sound of the crashing utensils, dogs began to bark, porch lights flashed on, and curtains were pulled back.

For a moment Abby and Joe stood frozen to the sidewalk in shock. Then Joe raised his eyes to the canopy of stars. "Not now. Please not *now*," he muttered in comically helpless frustration.

Abby felt hysteria rising in her. Then, unable to stop herself, she began to laugh silently, smothering the sound behind both hands. But when she caught a glimpse of the look on Joe's face, any attempt to disguise her amusement became futile.

As the dogs from the next street joined the raucous chorus, Joe began to chuckle, reluctantly at first, as though he couldn't help it, then in a mighty rumble that joined the other sounds. Abby doubled over weakly, leaning against his shaking body to keep from falling.

Suddenly a voice penetrated their laughter, a stern sound that came from the house next to Abby's.

"Everything's all right, Mrs. Rappaport," Abby said in a weak, unsteady voice. "Go back to bed."

"What did she say?" Joe whispered against her ear, puzzlement warring with amusement.

It was several seconds before she felt calm enough to whisper back, "Something about a dry morsel and quietness being better than sacrifices with strife."

"What on earth does it mean?"

Pulling herself up straight, she inhaled deeply to overcome the laughter she could feel bubbling up again. "Nobody questions Mrs. Rappaport. You just look thoughtful and nod your head."

He placed a hand on each side of her waist, holding her still until she glanced up at him inquiringly. Staring down at her, he smiled wistfully. "I suppose that puts an end to my coming inside?"

The regret that flooded her body overwhelmed her with its intensity. She leaned into him as he bent down to kiss her chastely on the cheek. "I'm afraid so," she murmured. "I guess—I guess it's for the best." She winced slightly when she heard the yearning in her voice.

"You don't believe that and neither do I," he said slowly, and for a breathless moment she was sure he was going to kiss her again. He leaned closer, then seemed to realize what was happening and pulled himself upright. Smiling wryly, he released her, then turned and waved casually toward the curtain that was pulled aside in the lighted window across the street before climbing back into his car.

Later, as she lay in bed, Abby couldn't get her mind off him. He had said he would teach her to have fun, but he hadn't told her she would be experiencing so many new and troubling emotions.

Why did she feel that she had the power to hurt him? she wondered. And why did she yearn so to protect him from that kind of hurt . . . from herself?

Six

Abby stared down at the apples and celery in the otherwise empty metal cart as she stood in the only grocery store in Bardle. She had been waiting for ten minutes in the checkout line of the Piggly-Wiggly Market, right behind Irene Betz, the banker's wife, and in front of Miss Cora Dunlap, retired secretary.

She knew from past experience that Irene and Georgette, the checker, would spend at least fifteen minutes talking about their gardens, making promises to swap rose moss for Wandering Jew, or bemoaning the voracious appetites of aphids.

Waiting didn't bother Abby. She had the patience that all small-town people acquire sooner or later out of self-defense, knowing that businesses could and did shut down completely if the cantaloupes needed picking or the crappie were biting.

For the past two days every time she had had a couple of unfilled minutes, her thoughts had turned inescapably to Joe. This time was no exception.

Early in the morning, the day after their

moonlight romp in the park, he had called to tell her he was leaving immediately for San Diego, where the national headquarters of his Shrimp Shacks company was located.

"Is this a genuine shrimp emergency?" she'd asked cheerfully, careful to hide the disappointment that suddenly overwhelmed her.

He had laughed then, but she'd heard the regret in his voice and it had warmed her. He had explained the emergency was more a matter of computers than shrimp and that he would be gone for several days.

During the past two days, even though he was out of town, Abby found she couldn't get away from Joe. When she was with her friends and neighbors, they talked about him incessantly. When she was alone, she thought of him constantly. And when she slept . . . when she slept, Abby dreamed of him longingly.

Oh, those dreams, she thought wildly. X-rated dreams. Dreams that should have made her blush, but didn't. And as though the blatant eroticism wasn't disturbing enough, there was something about them that was even more disquieting, something she couldn't come to grips with. The dreams were not about the present. They were about the future, a future with Joe firmly entrenched in her life.

It was that element she fought every morning when she awoke. In her conscious mind she knew she was satisfied with her life just as it was. And she knew that even if she wanted to marry, it would require an exceptional man to take on a ready-made family.

These objections were reality. But even reality

couldn't stop the incredible dreams. It bothered her that she might be unconsciously dissatisfied with her life. Why should she be yearning for something beyond her reach, something that could probably never be? Abby wondered.

Suddenly the line moved forward. Abby pushed her shopping cart forward and into the opening between the counter and the cash register.

"Morning, Abby," Georgette said, smiling broadly. "How are Brennie and Jeff getting on? Have they put any new gray hairs on your folks' heads yet?" As one who thoroughly enjoyed a good joke, especially her own, Georgette chuckled heartily as she stooped to lift the celery and apples out of the cart. "This is pretty sick-looking celery," she said. "It must be from out of state." She glanced up suddenly. "Speaking of foreigners, I hear our celebrity is out of town for a few days. I bet you're missing him, aren't you?"

Abby simply smiled and nodded. Denying that she and Joe were an item didn't work. She had tried it too many times already.

"I guess your boy Jeff is pretty excited," the thin brunette continued.

"I think everyone is excited about having Joe in town, Georgette," Abby replied calmly, ignoring the implications of her remark.

"For sure," Georgette said, nodding her head wisely. "But Jeff especially, poor skinny little thing. A boy shouldn't have to do without a father. He needs someone to teach him how to be a man."

"Georgette—" Abby began in exasperation, then stopped when Miss Cora, still standing behind Abby, leaned forward to interrupt their conversation.

"She's right, Abby," the elderly spinster said knowingly. "Jeff's getting a little wild."

"Wild?" Abby asked, concerned. "What do you mean, he's getting wild?"

What had her son being doing? she worried. Thoughts of a gang of ten-year-olds who went around terrorizing little old ladies began forming in her mind. When had he had time to participate in these wild escapades?

"The day that school let out he rang my doorbell three times," Miss Cora went on, shaking her gray head censoriously. "And then he hid in the bushes every time I answered the door."

Abby drew a relieved breath and shook her head. "I'm sorry, Miss Cora. I know that was annoying for you. I promise I'll talk to him about it."

"A father," she said firmly. "That's what the boy needs. You mark my words, he's headed straight for trouble."

Today doorbells; tomorrow bank vaults, Abby thought, hiding her grin. She turned back to Georgette, who gave her a sympathetic smile.

"He's a good boy," the checker said loyally. "But he must feel different from the other boys. And besides," she added, winking mischievously as she bagged Abby's purchases, "a woman alone is not a good thing. She dries up real fast." She glanced over at Miss Cora as though predicting that Abby would end up like the elderly woman if she didn't do something very soon.

Too much, Abby moaned silently as she put her small sack of groceries on the backseat of the station wagon. Why had everyone suddenly decided to marry her off? In the beginning it had been funny, but enough was enough already. Her sense of humor, not to mention her patience, was wearing very thin these days. How on earth could she and Joe enjoy a nice, simple flirtation if the whole town expected them to announce wedding plans at any minute?

Abby shook her head in exasperation, then parked the station wagon in front of Jensen's Pharmacy, and two doors down from Alberta's Cut and Curl—whose sign proclaimed it "The Best Little Hair House in Texas."

The small, air-conditioned pharmacy was thankfully empty of shoppers, and she wandered through the aisles, finally picking up a new lipstick and a large bottle of vitamins. Then she walked to the back of the store where the cash register was located.

"Good morning, Howard," she said to the white-smocked pharmacist.

"Well, hello, Abby," he said, peering around a shelf filled with hundreds of mysterious bottles and jars. "Is this all you need?" He stepped over and took the items from her and began to ring them up. "I guess you're a little at loose ends these days, what with Brennie and Jeff off at Sally and John's and now Joe going out of town." He paused to smile at her. "You got a real good man there, Abby. Better not let him get away."

Suffering succotash, she thought wildly. *Not again.*

"Howard," she said quietly and slowly through clenched teeth. "In all the television commercials the pharmacists are nice little gray-haired men who enthusiastically push Preparation-H, fluoride toothpaste, and gentle, overnight laxatives. It's a good system. Why tamper with success? Why is it that I'm the only person in the world whose druggist pushes used quarterbacks?"

She left the drugstore followed by the sound of Howard's loud, indulgent laughter. On the street she saw three of her neighbors heading in her direction, sparks of divine inspiration brightening their faces as they spotted her and hurried toward her eagerly. Abby moaned, this time audibly. Ducking quickly into her car, she waved gaily as she pulled out and headed for home, wondering if the whole world was conspiring against her.

When she reached her small frame house, she hurried inside, feeling a little as though she had been through a battle. Bloody, she thought, but unbowed.

Well, maybe a little bent, she added silently. She wanted to lock all the doors and windows and hibernate until everyone forgot about her and Joe. But she knew it wasn't possible. She had promised Judy she would join Harrison and her for lunch.

"I'll go," she muttered under her breath as she entered her bedroom to change into dusty green slacks and a matching cap-sleeved cotton blouse. "I'll go, but if one more person mentions him, I'll scream."

An hour later, as she rang Judy and Harrison's doorbell, she was still determined to steer any conversation away from Joe. But it seemed she had worried for nothing. Judy led her through the house to the backyard, chattering as usual, but without saying one word about Joe.

Then Abby realized why. As she walked

through the patio door, she saw him. The man who had been so constantly in her thoughts was sitting at a redwood picnic table between two of her friends, a look of harassed desperation on his rugged face as they both talked ninety miles a minute at him.

Her irritation fled magically. It was replaced by a burst of excitement and, she admitted silently, perhaps a little malicious amusement because now it was happening to him. Her friends and neighbors were apparently giving him the same treatment they had been giving her.

He rose quickly when he saw her enter the large, tree-shaded yard, and moved hurriedly to her side. Grasping her arm, he urged her away from the group—who all exchanged pleased glances—stopping only when he had put a large oak between them and her friends.

"Abby," he said in relief. "I thought you'd never get here."

"Do you still think you can outwit the people of Bardle?" she asked, laughing.

"They're like nothing I've ever come across," he said, shaking his head ruefully. "The tenacity and single-mindedness of the people of this town are mind-boggling."

"I take it you're as sick of hearing about Abby as I am of hearing about Joe?"

"No, no," he objected. "I love hearing about you. It's just the look they get in their eyes. It makes me feel like a stud bull they're all trying to corral."

"A stud bull?" she murmured with a small, inquisitive smile. She reached out to play with a button on his shirt, glancing up at him through her lashes as she said sweetly, "I take it I'm the cow that's waiting to be serviced."

He burst out laughing, his eyes coming vibrantly alive as he leaned closer. "I didn't mean that . . . although it certainly presents some interesting possibilities," he added thoughtfully. "It's just that I had planned on wooing you a little less publicly."

"Wooing me?" she asked with a chuckle. "Is that what you've been doing?"

"Do you doubt it?" Although he didn't move, he seemed closer, and she could feel his breath on her cheeks.

It suddenly became very difficult for Abby to catch her breath and she realized just how much she had missed him, how much she had missed the excitement that sang through her blood when she was near him. As she stared at his face, at his lips, the low rumble of voices in the yard faded away completely. All that was left was the glorious sunshine, the sound of a single mockingbird . . . and Joe.

"I called you earlier," he said softly. "I wanted to tell you I was back, but you weren't home."

She cleared her throat to make sure it still worked. "I—I had a few things to pick up . . . I'm sorry I missed your call," she told him in an almost inaudible whisper.

"So am I. And I'm sorry we're here and I'm sorry I can't take you in my arms to remind you what it feels like." His voice was low and husky and sent tiny shivers coursing through her body, making her light-headed.

For a few seconds they simply stared into each other's eyes, communicating silently. But all too soon the others in the backyard began protesting, refusing to be excluded from their wordless conversation, and they reluctantly rejoined the small group.

"Hello, Abby."

She turned when she heard the voice behind her, and lifted her eyes heavenward at the teasing grin on the familiar masculine face. Then her gaze immediately skimmed to the man standing behind him to take in an identical grin on an almost identical face.

"Aren't you going to introduce us to your friend?" Larry Kestler asked smugly, recognizing the wariness of Abby's expression.

She turned back to Joe and said in resignation, "Joe, meet Larry and Roy Kestler. As you can see, they're identical twins . . . and I'll warn you right now, they have identically warped minds." As Joe stretched to shake hands with her redheaded, freckle-faced friends, she added spitefully, "I call them Bric and Brac because they're always together and are both so amazingly inconsequential."

"And we love you too," Roy said, throwing his arm around her to give her a brotherly squeeze. He glanced at Joe and pulled his Huckleberry Finn face into stern lines. "Now, Mr. Gilbraithe, we'd like to know just what your intentions are regarding our Abigail."

"Roy! Will you shut up?" she said in exasperation. Turning to Joe, she added, "Pay no attention to them. I've known them both since kindergarten, and believe me, it's the only way to handle them."

Larry wiggled his bushy eyebrows and bent

over, Groucho-style. "I can think of a few other ways you could handle me, but you always say no."

"Marsha," Roy shouted, glancing over to where Larry's wife was talking to Judy. "Larry's talking dirty again."

"Come here, darling," Marsha called. Then, to no one in particular, she added, "Isn't he adorable?"

"Are they always like that?" Joe asked as the twins walked away.

"This is one of their quiet days," she said. "Wait until school starts. Harrison spent two months last year trying to find out which student put the panties over the head of the statue in front of the school, only to discover it was Larry and Roy."

"They teach?"

She nodded. "Geometry and algebra. Remarkably, they're very good teachers and the kids adore them." As they walked toward the group at the table to the accompaniment of the devilish grins of the twins, she added, "Probably because they have mentalities similar to those of their students."

Joe sat beside Abby on one side of a long redwood table, not even listening as she chatted idly with her friends while they all ate charcoal-broiled hamburgers and baked beans. He was itching to be alone with her and, irrationally, felt impatient with these people for being there.

It seemed like years since he had touched her, held her. The whole time he'd been in California she'd been in his thoughts. Even during the day, when he should have been concentrating on business, he would suddenly find himself thinking of something she had done or said. Or simply remembering the way her lake-green eyes sparkled when she smiled.

He glanced over at her now and, without giving himself time to think, slipped one foot out of his leather sandal, moving it slowly until it found hers.

Suddenly Abby felt Joe's bare foot on top of hers, caressing it softly. For a moment she felt the urge to laugh; then, as awareness filled her, she held herself perfectly still to keep the shiver of pleasure rippling through her from showing.

Glancing at him from beneath her lashes, she caught an impudent grin on his face. When he slid his foot up to tickle her under the hem of her slacks, then moved it down again, she slipped off her own shoe. Lifting her foot slowly, she curled her toes around the hair on his shin and yanked.

Joe's yelp of pain was drowned in his iced tea and he began to choke, but he waved Larry away when the twin began to pound him on the back with good-natured heartiness.

"That's a cute trick," Joe whispered, darting her a surreptitious and slightly vengeful glance. "What else do you do with your toes?"

She gave him a seductive smile and leaned closer. "Lots of things. I also"—she ran one finger softly over the large, tanned hand that rested on the table—"pick up pencils with them."

Everyone turned to stare when Joe began to chuckle, and he once again turned his attention to his baked beans. He patiently gossiped with the group around the table, bemoaning the lack of rain and the overabundance of inefficient politicians. Each second that he could endure brought him closer to being alone with Abby.

"You really think you can pull it off?" Roy directed his question to Joe. The remains of lunch had been cleared away and they were now sitting in a cluster of lawn chairs under the shade of a large mimosa.

"You don't even know what kind of players we'll have this year," Roy went on. "Our best man was injured about a week ago."

"Who was injured?" Abby asked in concern. "I didn't hear anything about it."

Roy grinned at her. "You've had other things on your mind, darling. Bubba Turner pulled a muscle while he was helping his father load watermelons. Doctor Harding said the leg would heal all right if he could just keep Bubba off it. But you know Bubba." He rolled his eyes and pointed to his head. "More brawn than brain."

"Look who's talking," she said dryly. "I'm sorry to hear about Bubba; he's a sweet boy."

"Well, Joe," Roy asked again. "What do you think?"

"I'm going to do my damnedest, Roy," Joe said, leaning forward in his chair. "If you think it would help, I could drop by and see Bubba. But even if he's out, I think we have a good chance. Like you said, I don't know the team, but I've been viewing some of the game films from last year. I think we may have some hidden talent."

"Who?" Larry, Roy, and Harrison all asked simultaneously, and identical curiosity burned in three pairs of eyes.

Joe laughed. "Be patient. You'll see soon enough."

He successfully dodged their questions and turned the conversation away from football. Later in the afternoon, when a decent time had elapsed after lunch, he signaled Abby it was time to leave. It took some fast talking on his part to get them away from her outgoing friends, but he eventually managed to convince them that they had to go.

"You've got a vicious streak," Abby said as they walked slowly, hand in hand, toward her house, "telling them that there was a superstar on the team whom everyone had overlooked. That was really mean."

"The end justifies the mean," he said with a wicked smile.

"Oh, that's bad," she moaned. "That's really bad. You should—"

"Aha!"

Abby turned her head toward the gruff voice to see Eb sitting on his porch. "Oh Lord," she muttered. "He's aha-ing again." She glanced at Joe. "Have you met our town philosopher yet?"

"No," he said cautiously. "I don't believe I have."

"Are you in for a treat," Abby said guilelessly, unable to keep a tiny gleam of humor out of her eyes. Pulling on his hand, she guided him up the walk to where Eb sat rocking in a straight-backed wooden rocker.

Before they had reached the steps, Eb called out, "Bubbling up, didn't I say so, Abby girl?" His shoulders bobbed up and down as he laughed in delight. "You two are a caution. I haven't had so much fun watching this town since Miss Cora Dunlap fell out of her window right smack into the middle of her rhododendrons while she was trying to get a better look at Ellen Thompson's new feathered hat."

"Eb, I'd like you to meet Joe Gilbraithe," Abby said, ignoring the amusement in the old man's alert blue eyes. "Joe, this is Ebenezer Watson. Watch out when you shake hands; he's probably got a joy buzzer."

"Abby, Abby," Eb said, shaking his head. "I can't believe—" He broke off abruptly and looked down at the ancient bloodhound lying at his feet. "Did you see that? Why, I never would have believed it."

Abby and Joe stared down at the dog as he lazily opened one eye, then closed it.

"See what?" Joe asked in bewilderment.

"The way he perked right up when he saw you," Eb said in amazement. "I've never seen Walter take to anyone so quicklike. Have you, Abby?"

Abby had to bite her lip to keep from laughing at the confused expression on Joe's face as he watched Walter yawn. She couldn't help him. All she could do was watch helplessly as Eb suckered him in.

"He . . . he doesn't seem very alert," Joe offered hesitantly.

"That's because Walter's deep," Eb said, watching the dog and nodding his head sagely. "Real deep. He spends a lot of time studying things."

"Eb," Abby said, laughing when she could hold back no longer. "You'd better be careful. Someone's going to strangle you one of these days."

"No, I reckon when I die it'll be because I been shot." He paused, glancing at them both with twinkling eyes. "By a jealous husband."

Even though she had heard Eb's bragging a

hundred times, Abby couldn't keep from chuckling again.

"So," Eb said, looking Joe over from top to bottom, "you're the one that's put our Abby in a tailspin."

"Eb," Abby gasped, shooting him a pleading look and trying to ignore the gleam of satisfaction that had appeared in Joe's dark eyes.

Eb gave her a pleased grin. "Old people can say anything they want to, girl. It's about the only good thing that goes with being old," he added wryly. "That and watching you young people going through the same blessed antics I went through fifty years ago." He paused to survey them both thoughtfully. "It's going to be mighty interesting seeing how this turns out. Yessir, mighty interesting."

Abby hurried Joe away to the sound of Eb's laughter. After a thoughtful moment during which Abby was afraid Joe was going to comment on Eb's blunt statements, he said, "Was he serious? About Walter, I mean."

"Yes, he was very serious about putting you on," she said, hiding a sigh of relief. "Don't be fooled by Eb's 'simple country folk' act. At one time he was a famous judge in these parts."

"A judge? No kidding." He glanced back toward Eb's house, a look of respect growing in his eyes.

She nodded. "He's one of the most intelligent men I've ever met, but he does enjoy a joke."

"I gathered that," Joe said, grinning. "I'd like to talk to him one of these days." He was silent for a moment; then, when they reached her front gate, he sighed heavily. "I like your friends, Abby. I really do."

"But—" she prompted.

"But I can't even play footsie with you without all of them watching us," he grumbled.

"Is playing footsie a big thing in your life?" she asked inquisitively.

"You know what I mean."

She nodded, her eyes wistful. "I know. I'm not even going to say I told you so, because I could use a break away from them myself."

"Let's run away from home," he suggested eagerly.

She laughed. "I don't think that would work. But maybe we could find a way to escape them that's a little less drastic." Suddenly a thought occurred to her and her green eyes brightened perceptibly. "Why didn't I think of it before? Tomorrow's First Monday."

"Tomorrow's Saturday," he said, eyeing her doubtfully.

"First Monday begins on Friday," she explained over her shoulder as she stepped up on the porch.

Coming to an abrupt halt, he took hold of her shoulders and turned her toward him. "Explain. What exactly is First Monday?"

"In Canton—a town to the east of here—they used to have a trade day on the first Monday of each month. Only it became so popular, they expanded it to include the weekend before. It's a giant flea market and carnival combined. I haven't been there in years."

"It sounds wonderful," he said with overdone enthusiasm.

"Well, maybe not wonderful," she said carefully, "but different anyway." She smiled up at him. "You showed me how to have fun in your world; now it's my turn to show you how we do it in mine."

"If it means we can get away from our chaperons for a while, it will be heaven." His smile faded as he stared down at her. "I don't want to leave," he said in a husky whisper, his hand moving slowly over the soft underside of her arm. "But I'm expecting a business call this evening." He glanced down at the sidewalk. "I don't suppose you would join me at my house," he suggested hopefully.

She shook her head vigorously. "Do you know how many people in this town own binoculars? This is my town and I love every single person in it, but gossip is the leading entertainment for most of them."

"That's what I was afraid of." He inhaled deeply and she could feel all his muscles tighten. His eyes took on the strangest look—intense and hungry. "Dammit, Abby. I want to kiss you. I want to hold you close, to feel you against me, to know the curve of your spine under my fingers, the softness of your belly under my face."

She drew her breath in sharply, unable to do anything more than stare at him in wide-eyed fascination as he continued.

"Do you realize we've never been completely alone? Someone is always there, waiting to interrupt us. I feel like a clumsy teenager trying to get his best girl away from her kid sister." He gave her a wistful look. "Why couldn't you have lived in a big, impersonal city?"

"We probably wouldn't have met," she said with a small, shaky laugh.

"Yes. We would have," he said emphatically. "I'm positive of that. Think of all the things that led up to our getting together. If any single incident had happened differently, we would have missed each other." He stared at her with a look of growing wonder, wonder that he was urging her to share. "But they didn't happen differently, Abby. Every step was just the one that was needed to get me to you."

Abby listened to him carefully as he spoke. The whole thing sounded magical the way he put it, and he didn't have to tell her that she would have missed something important if she had never met him. She wanted very much to believe what he was saying, but she was too unsure of how man-woman games were played. Was this a part of it? Was she reading more into it than he intended?

Joe was an honorable man, she thought. She would stake her life on that, but how could she be sure that this type of talk was not an ordinary part of the mating game?

Don't make a fool of yourself, her good sense urged her. *Don't let your dreams push aside reality.*

"Joe—" she began hesitantly.

"Don't," he said, cutting her off abruptly. "Don't look ahead. I'm not demanding anything of you, am I?"

She shook her head silently, but her gray-green eyes were still wary.

"Then don't worry about it. All I ask is that you don't shut me out. Let things happen the way they happen." He lifted her chin. "Okay?"

She inhaled slowly, then smiled. "Sure. Why not? I've got three weeks left to be footloose and fancy free." She glanced up at him and added, "And for that time, I'm all yours, quarterback."

He didn't comment. Instead he raised a hand to touch his mouth with his index finger, then brought the finger to her lips in a soft caress, pulling at the tender flesh to find the moist inner lip. It was the most breathtakingly erotic promise she had ever received.

Her eyes slowly shut, opening only after he had withdrawn his hand and begun to walk away. As she watched him, her own words rose up to plague her.

I'm all yours, quarterback.

Seven

Joe arrived at Abby's front door before eight the next morning, feeling a little like he had as a kid when he had played hooky from school. When she opened the front door and stepped out, his eyes ran slowly over the long, tanned legs that her white shorts set off perfectly.

"You know, I really love your legs," he said as she turned back to pick up a big straw hat. "After your smile, they were probably the first thing I noticed about you."

She smiled. "Do you want to know the first thing I noticed about you?"

"Let me think about that a minute," he said ruefully. "You have a way of knocking my ego flat." He paused, more to listen to the sound of her laughter than to think. "Was it my majestic nose?"

"No," she said, shaking her head. "It was your eyes."

"You like my eyes?"

"Yes, I do. But that's not what I meant. You kept them trained on my legs from the minute I walked into Harrison's house." She eyed him solemnly. "I thought maybe you had some kind of astigmatism."

"You see what I mean?" he said, laughing. "Come on, woman. Let's leave before you try to twist the knife."

He started to pull the door closed behind her, but didn't quite manage to do it before Merry flew through the small opening. Before he could do more than blink, the dog had bounded down the walk and jumped through the open window into the backseat of the car.

"Merry," Abby said in exasperation as she walked to the car. "Get out."

Joe lifted the dog out of the car and started back toward the house, but the squirming animal was impossible to hold. Seconds later he watched helplessly as Merry ran through his legs and took his place in the backseat again. The feisty animal seemed to grin as he watched Joe and Abby walk toward him in frustration.

Joe smiled wryly, glancing down at Abby. "As I was saying, what we really need on this trip is a dog."

Abby stopped short. "You don't mean to take him?" she asked in disbelief.

"Why not? He'll probably enjoy the trip."

"Oh, I don't doubt that a bit," she said dryly. "I just wonder how much we'll enjoy it with him along."

He gave her a coaxing smile. "Aw, come on, Abby. Let him come with us."

She shrugged in wary resignation. "You'll be sorry," she said, then turned back to the house. "At least let me get his leash. We can't let him run loose and it's too hot to leave him in the car."

Abby was still throwing menacing looks at the happy animal in the backseat when they turned onto the back road that would take them to I-20 and then to Canton.

Joe caught her eye as she turned back to watch the road ahead. "Did you talk to the kids last night?" he asked casually.

"Uh-huh." She smiled. "I told them I would call once a week, but I'm afraid it's been more like three times a week."

"Are they having a good time?"

"They love staying with my parents," she said quietly, then more enthusiastically, "You're going to love Canton, Joe. Once a month the whole town goes crazy."

He knew she was changing the subject purposely, and he had to fight the hurt that welled up inside him. He wondered suddenly if she was even conscious of what she was doing. She didn't want to talk about her children because she wasn't ready to let him in yet.

Keeping his eyes on the road, he decided not to push. Not yet, anyway. "It sounds like you're looking forward to it."

"I am," she agreed. "It's wonderful, but only if you're a people person. In the last decade, First Monday has taken over the whole town. Sometimes you have to walk half a mile from where you park your car to get to the trade grounds, but that's all part of the fun."

Abby leaned back and relaxed. She hoped Joe would appreciate her idea of fun. If nothing else, she thought, it would certainly be a new experience for him.

Twisting in her seat, she studied his strangely

solemn face. "Do you realize you've only been in Bardle for about six weeks?" She shook her head. "It doesn't seem possible. Sometimes I feel I've known you all my life."

He smiled, the somber expression disappearing. "It happens that way sometimes. Maybe our souls are very old and knew each other in past lives."

"There are times, usually on a Monday morning in the middle of the school year, when my soul feels as old as Methuselah." Abby paused, listening to the sound of his laughter. "But if you discount the old souls theory, don't you think it's strange that two people with such different backgrounds can think and feel so much alike?" Before he could answer, she added, "I'm talking about how we laugh at the same things and get angry at the same things. I've always wondered how much cultures have to do with mind processes."

"We didn't have a lot of culture in my area of Brooklyn," he said, grinning. "Environment versus heredity? I'm not a biologist or an anthropologist, but I know that you can take two people—even people with the same parents—put them in the same environment, and they'll turn out different. I've wondered about that before. In my neighborhood the only successful people, the role models, you might say, were pushers and pimps. So why did I secretly ache to be the all-American jock?" He shrugged, then continued in a quiet, thoughtful voice. "I'm glad it worked out the way it did, but I don't understand it. I guess there are some things that will never be explained by science."

Suddenly he gave her a startled look. "We're

supposed to be having a holiday. How did we get off on such a deep subject?"

She laughed. "As a matter of fact, I started it, but I was just trying to tell you that I like you."

"And trying to figure out why?" he asked wryly.

"No," she said, grinning. "I know why."

"Oh?"

"Sure," she said, nodding seriously. "You're the only source of free shrimp I have."

Growling fiercely, he pulled her across the seat and held her close to him in what was intended to be a punishment, but in actuality suited her just fine.

The small town of Canton lay an hour east of Dallas and about ten miles south of the interstate highway, on the edge of the piney woods. On the weekends of First Monday people came by the thousands from all over Texas to wander through the multitude of booths and tents that offered everything from designer clothes to plastic clocks.

When they arrived, Abby could see that Joe was a little taken aback and overwhelmed by the exuberant country-fair atmosphere, but it didn't take him much time to get into the swing of things. Before long he was acting like the regulars, treating each person they met as though he were a lifelong friend.

Joe and Abby wandered by hundreds of booths. They stopped to hear guitars and portable organs demonstrated, and to examine dolls with exquisite porcelain faces and handmade clothing, marveling over junk and antiques alike. They agreed that their favorite booth was the one that displayed beautifully stitched handmade quilts, the patterns for which had been handed down from generation to generation. Abby could have stayed for hours, but eventually Merry insisted they move on.

Joe smiled at an old man in overalls, then glanced down at Abby. Did she know? he wondered. Could she tell he felt on the outside looking in? He loved her world, the easygoing, friendly attitude of the people he met. But he wasn't a part of it. He was only a visitor, an outsider.

All his life he had felt different from the rest of the world, different from "normal" people, and that difference was a line he couldn't seem to cross.

Even when he had been on top in football, the estrangement had been there. People had fought to be his "friends," but only because he was a celebrity. He felt that up until the time he'd come to Bardle, Harrison had been the only one who saw him as a real person.

Now there was Abby. Sometimes he felt that if he ever decided to show her just how much she meant to him, he would scare her off. He wanted so desperately to be a part of her world, a real part. The only problem was, he didn't quite know how to accomplish that. He couldn't just barge in and say "here I am," he thought. She had to invite him in. She had to want him in as badly as he wanted to be there.

Suddenly he laughed, putting his thoughtful mood aside as he saw Merry do a quick U-turn toward a hot dog stand. Food was everywhere and the smell was irresistible, to them as well as to the dog.

Heroically they tried steak sandwiches piled high with sautéed onions, and for dessert, frozen pureed fruit on a stick. Then, carrying huge, sun-ripened peaches, they wandered away from the crowded fairgrounds, running hand in hand up a small hill. Laughing and out of breath, they sat under a huge oak at the top, where the raucous country music drifted up to them along with the summer breeze.

While Merry curled up to take a nap, Abby leaned against the tree and watched Joe finish his peach with greedy relish. She grinned as the juice ran unhampered down his chin.

"Something funny?" he asked, leaning closer with a wicked gleam in his eyes.

"Joe, don't you dare," she said in alarm as she backed away. Then suddenly she was caught in his iron grasp and his lips found hers in a kiss that was different from anything she had ever experienced.

The sensation should have been comic, and at first she did have the urge to laugh; then something extraordinary happened. The wet sweetness and the delicious slippery warmth of his lips caused a mini-explosion inside her. Her breathing became labored as she urged her body closer to his and began to suck at his lips, his tongue.

For a moment Joe held himself still, as though in shock; then a groan came from deep within his chest and he pushed her back onto the grass and covered her body with his.

Arching her hips to meet the hardness of his groin, Abby clung tightly to his neck, digging her fingers into the taut tendons as she moved against him.

"Abby, Abby," he murmured against her lips. "My God, what are you trying to do to me?"

She couldn't speak. His body felt so good against her, hard, tough strength pushing into her softness, making her feel desired, and more womanly than she could ever remember feeling.

Everything around them disappeared into a kind of vague mist. For Abby there was only his mouth, his tongue probing insistently, demanding that she give and take freely. She felt she would die for the feel of his lips on hers.

Suddenly loud laughter penetrated the sensual bands that held them and Abby blinked in surprise. "Good grief! What happened?" she gasped, then rolled from beneath him to sit up and stare at him with stunned eyes.

He sat up slowly and wrapped his arms around his knees, but not before she had seen the result of her actions. After a moment he shook his head and gave a dazed laugh. "I don't know," he said slowly, his voice hoarse. "But I think I'm going to stock up on peaches."

With a startled burst of laughter, she said, "Joe, I'm sorry. I don't know what came over me."

He stared at her in silence for a moment. "Don't apologize, Abby. Whatever happened, it was honest. Don't ever be sorry for being honest. Not with me."

She nodded slowly, then smiled, feeling every bit of her embarrassment slip away with his sincere words. When she leaned back against a tree, he moved to lay his head in her lap and she spent a satisfying few minutes playing with his thick, springy hair.

"I wonder," she said lazily, "if you know how much you're admired by the people in Bardle . . . especially now that people have gotten to know you. At first they saw you only as a superstar, with their mouths hanging open in awe. Now they consider you one of them, and you can just see them all bursting with pride."

He gave her an odd glance, then after a moment said, "That's flattering, but I'm really just an ordinary man who happened to fall into a job where I was highly visible."

"Ordinary?" she said skeptically. "What about your work with the Special Olympics?" She paused thoughtfully. "Did you get involved with those kids because of your background? Because you considered yourself handicapped?"

He shrugged. "That could have been part of it, but it was really just one of those things that sneak up on you before you know it.

"I was watching television one Sunday." He stared up into the leaves of the tree and at the pieces of sky in between, speaking softly and slowly. "Just passing the time until the football game came on. The station was showing some clips from a local Special Olympics. You've probably seen clips like it. All those kids . . ." His voice trailed away. Then he cleared his throat and continued. "It wasn't long before I forgot all about the football game. I was totally involved with those kids. But no more, I suppose, than any other person would be. Anyway, after several events they had a sprint race. All the kids seemed so proud just to be participating. While they were milling around before the race, I noticed this kid in a wheelchair. I didn't really pay much attention to him. He was just another of the hundreds that tear at your heart. I didn't realize then that he had entered the race."

He was silent for so long, Abby was beginning to think he was not going to continue, but then he went on. "When the race started, the camera concentrated mostly on the kids in front. Then suddenly it panned behind those kids and there was the boy in the wheelchair, slowly wheeling his chair down the track. He—" Joe stopped to inhale slowly, but his voice remained raspy and harsh. "Abby, he couldn't even hold his head upright."

She heard an indecipherable emotion—almost anger—in his voice and could tell the words were more difficult for him now.

"Well," he said in a gust, "the race didn't last long. The winner and runners-up were congratulating each other and being hugged by friends. There was a lot of excitement all around. Then the camera cut back and the boy in the wheelchair was still on the track . . . slowly moving those wheels. He wasn't even halfway through." He closed his eyes. "The race was over and he was still moving that damn chair. About then the crowd started clapping in time, urging him on. I found myself beating my fists on the arms of my chair as though somehow he could see me, hear me. People were standing up, hanging over the rails, screaming encouragement." He paused to take a deep breath. "And dammit, Abby, he made it. He pushed that metal obscenity over the finish line and the crowd went wild . . . and so did I. I sat there with both fists raised in victory, crying like a baby. I felt drained, as though I'd been pushing that damn chair myself." He stared up at her. "But you know, there was no pity. Those kids didn't deserve my pity. Only admiration and pride because they're America's children, the world's children. But I also felt shame. Shame because I had let so many small things get to me."

He shook his head. "I couldn't watch that kind of courage and not be a part of it," he finished simply.

Abby sat perfectly still for a long time, letting waves of emotion wash over her. She knew there were tears on her face, but she didn't care. She didn't try to speak; she merely bent down slowly and kissed his cheeks, his eyes. Then she held his head in her hands as she kissed his mouth.

It was a special moment, one she knew she would remember for the rest of her life. And, although Abby didn't recognize it yet, she had finally let Joe in.

Leaning back against the tree, she smoothed his hair lovingly. They stayed as they were until late afternoon, then silently stood and walked back to the car.

The road they took to get back to I-20 was narrow but paved, and wound through miles and miles of woods. Abby leaned against Joe, content just to watch the passing scenery.

"Are you thinking about getting back to Bardle?" he asked quietly.

"Actually, I was trying to avoid thinking about that," she said, smiling. "It's been such a wonderful day. I hate to see it—" A noise from the back seat interrupted her.

Merry had been asleep since they left Canton, but suddenly he began to whine. Abby glanced over her shoulder just as he started to scratch frantically on the back door.

"Oh dear," she murmured warily. "Joe, I think

you'd better pull over. That scratching is awfully familiar."

When he stopped the car, Abby reattached the leash to Merry's collar and stepped out. Luckily the area beside the road wasn't fenced and she began to follow the dog to the edge of the trees.

"Isn't nature wonderful?" Joe said, laughing as he walked beside her.

"Sure," she said dryly, then, as the dog sniffed at another tree and passed it by, "Merry, for heaven's sake, don't be so picky."

Suddenly the leash was jerked from her hand and Merry disappeared into the woods. Abby turned her startled gaze toward Joe.

He shrugged. "Maybe he spotted the perfect tree."

"Merry!" she called in exasperation, then started to move in the direction the dog had taken.

"Shouldn't we wait here for him?" Joe asked, catching her arm as she went past him.

"You don't know Merry," Abby said. "And you don't know the guilt a ten-year-old boy can lay on you with one look. If I lose Merry, I might as well look for a new home." She shook her head. "I'm telling you the kid has expressions that would break a heart of stone."

Suddenly she caught a glimpse of a white, wagging tail. "There he is!" she cried as she took off after him.

"Abby," Joe called as he followed her, "I really don't think this is a good idea."

Fifteen minutes later she was forced to agree with Joe. The playful dog was letting them see him just often enough to keep the chase going. When he disappeared again, Abby leaned against a tree to catch her breath, cursing softly.

Joe stood beside her, looking around at the solid wall of trees. "I'm sure glad you know this place, because I have no idea where we are."

Abby looked at him for a moment, then up at the sky, but she didn't say anything.

"Abby," he began tentatively when the silence began to lengthen. "You do know this place, don't you?"

"Actually . . ." she said hesitantly.

"You mean we're lost?" For a moment she thought he was going to explode. Then he began to laugh. "I never knew country life could be so exciting."

She glanced up at him, her expression defensive. "Well, you seemed so at home on our camping trip, I figured you would know how to find the way back."

He gave another yelp of laughter. "I'm from *Brooklyn*, Abby. Do you know what that means? It means that sick-looking weeds growing through cracks in the cement is the closest I came to a forest for most of my life."

"But you've had plenty of time to explore the wonderful world of the outdoors since you left Brooklyn."

"And I have," he agreed, still chuckling. "But it's always been in civilized camping grounds or with a guide. This is not civilized"—he waved a hand at their surroundings—"and we have no guide."

Suddenly Merry appeared beside them, his tongue lolling, his tail wagging in contentment. Abby looked down at him with venom in her eyes.

"Merry dear, do you know how close you were to being an ex-dog? Now, come on, sweetheart, show us the way back to the car."

Merry barked as though he understood every word and suddenly took off through the trees. Abby and Joe followed close behind as the small dog successively flushed out a rabbit, a quail, and several field larks before they decided it was a losing proposition.

"Now what?" Joe asked, his voice sounding strange as his body shook with laughter.

"Well, laughing certainly isn't going to accomplish anything," she said, throwing him a disgruntled look. "How do I know what we're going to do? I suppose you want me to cut down a tree and carve a jeep—"

She broke off and gave him a sheepish smile when he hugged her to him. "Oh, Joe. What *are* we going to do? It's beginning to get dark."

"Are there bears in Texas?"

She drew back sharply. "Did you have to say that? I don't even like frogs and you talk about bears." She paused thoughtfully. "Did you know that frogs have teeth?"

"I promise I won't let any frogs eat you," he said solemnly. "Look, we headed west when we left the car, so if we keep what's left of the sun behind us, we should eventually come to the road."

Reaching down to get the end of Merry's leash, he began to lead them in an easterly direction. Twilight seemed to fall very quickly, and just when she felt things couldn't get worse, Abby felt a drop of rain on her cheek. She heard Joe's muttered curse, then suddenly a surprised exclamation.

"What is it?"

"I don't know," he said. "Some kind of structure." He glanced down at her. "Abby, I think we'd better check it out . . . just in case."

"You think we may have to spend the night here?"

"I'm afraid so, love. The rain is beginning to come down harder. Come on, let's see what it is."

The structure he had spotted had been a cabin once upon a time. Now it was nothing more than a pile of boards that seemed to be held together only by the sheer willpower of the lumber.

"It looks like a place where bats hold their conventions," Abby said warily, eyeing the disreputable-looking place. Suddenly she shivered. "Joe, I really hate spiders and snakes."

"Why don't you stay out here under the eaves with Merry while I go in and look around?"

She didn't even feel cowardly as she nodded and handed him the lighter she carried in her pocket. Once he had entered the cabin, the minutes passed slowly. She jumped skittishly when a loud crash came from inside, but before she could go after him, Joe appeared again in the doorway.

"It's not exactly the Ritz, but it will keep the wolves off us," he said as he led her inside.

"Wolves? Did you say wolves?"

"I'm just teasing," he said, chuckling. Waving a hand around them, he asked, "Well, what do you think?"

He was right, she thought. It wasn't the Ritz. But somehow he had managed to light a fire in the ancient fireplace and to pull a lumpy old mattress before it.

Merry needed no further invitation. He briskly

shook the water off his coat, curled up on the hearth, and fell asleep.

"His conscience certainly doesn't seem to be bothering him," Abby muttered as she moved closer to the fire. She shivered until the warmth began to penetrate her damp clothing, then turned to look at Joe as he poked around in the dusty cabin. "I guess it could have been worse," she said. "It could have rained a lot harder and we could have been stuck out—"

She broke off abruptly as a sharp pain attacked her leg.

"What's wrong?"

"A cramp in my leg," she said, laughing and moaning at the same time. "I hate it when it does this. I can feel my toes curling up and there's nothing I can do to stop it."

"Come here. Lie down and I'll fix it for you. If there's one thing I learned during my years as a football player, it's what to do for muscle cramps."

She regarded him warily as she sat down on the mattress. "You will remember that I'm not a linebacker, won't you?"

He laughed. "Trust me." He pushed her back and turned her over on her stomach. "You can safely put your leg in my hands."

He fell silent and the only sounds in the small cabin for the next few minutes were Abby's sighs. Then suddenly he rolled her over, a look of amazement crossing his features.

"Abby," he said excitedly. "We're alone!"

She stared at him for a moment. "Yes," she said slowly. "We're alone. I think that's a good thing. Out here the only company we might get would probably want to have us for dinner."

He laughed, shaking his head. "You don't understand. For the first time since I've known you there is absolutely no possibility that we could be interrupted. No neighbors will come barging in. No friends will check to see how we're getting along."

"You poor thing," she said, chuckling. "You haven't gotten a very favorable taste of small-town living, have you? I agree that there's not much chance for privacy, but that's only one side of the coin. On the other side is the fact that you never have to face problems alone. Everyone pitches in to help during the bad times."

She could see that she still hadn't convinced him; his eyes hadn't lost their avid sparkle.

"I feel like doing something really wild," he said, as though she hadn't spoken.

"Like what?" she asked, her eyes narrowing.

"Oh, I don't know. Something completely reckless, something I couldn't do in Bardle."

"You want to write dirty words on the walls?"

He threw back his head and laughed, then plopped down beside her and pulled her into his arms. "Abby," he said slowly, staring down at her startled face, "I'm going to kiss you. I'm going to kiss you to within an inch of your life, the way I've been wanting to for weeks."

"Joe, this is not the old follow-the-dog-into-the-woods-and-get-her-lost trick, is it?" she asked warily. "Because if it is, I refuse—"

Her protest was stopped by his descending mouth and, after the first surprised moment, she completely forgot about protesting and slid into the unbelievable pleasure of his kiss.

As she felt a fiery ache growing in her loins, Abby understood at last what had happened to her under the tree in Canton. She had wanted Joe, wanted him desperately for a long time, but had managed to hide her need even from herself.

Her feverish movement against him was a conscious cry for more. And as he touched her with his hands, his mouth, Abby felt she would never be whole, never be a complete woman, until she was truly his.

With his hand cupping her breast, he lowered his lips into the opening of her blouse, straining to touch as much of her warm flesh as he could. She could feel the strength of his desperate desire pressed against her and ached to feel him inside her.

When he raised his head to look down at her, the desperate, hungry look had returned to his eyes. "You understand, don't you?" he whispered. "It's not a game anymore. It hasn't been for a long time."

As he talked, he slid his hand between her panties and her skin, just the fingertips at first, then more, until he could spread his fingers across her rounded stomach, so close to the center of her aching need.

Abby reached up to pull his mouth back to hers, but he held back slightly. "If you want to stop me, babe, it will have to be now," he said huskily.

This was the moment Abby had dreamed of so often. It was a moment she had almost feared, but now, faced with the reality, there was no hesitation in her.

"Please," she whispered softly. Releasing her hold on his neck, she moved her hand to unbutton the first button on his shirt.

The primitive flame that leaped into his dark

eyes burned into her. It scorched her body at the core of her desire. It scorched her heart. And as they slowly undressed each other, it burned wildly out of control until each breath seared her nostrils and her throat.

At last she was free to touch every inch of him. She lovingly explored each of the scars that marked his years in football. His heated flesh felt wonderfully vibrant under her caressing fingers, her wandering lips. And when she buried her face in his hard belly, a groan of pleasure escaped him, making her wild with desire.

She ached for him and at that moment she felt she would do anything for the love of him. She felt faint with the intensity of the sensations she was experiencing as he branded her body with his greedy hands, his insatiable mouth.

When he entered her at last, she arched to meet him eagerly. It was the fulfillment of a dream, and as her world shook at the indescribably sweet sensation, an indecipherable cry of ecstasy escaped her.

This was where her life had been leading, Abby thought. She believed that now. He filled her completely, becoming a part of her. Each touch, each kiss, was unbearably perfect. His cries of pleasure were food to her hungry heart.

And just before the sky opened and allowed a little bit of heaven to shine on them, she knew that she had been irrevocably changed by the man in her arms.

For a long time they simply lay still, the firelight flickering on their naked bodies as they clung together. Then Joe began to speak, his voice barely a whisper, intense and low.

"Ever since I was a kid I've had a problem falling asleep at night. And sometimes in the middle of the night, too often for comfort, I would wake up suddenly, my heart pounding in my chest as if I had just run a race." He stared into the fire, stroking the long line of her hip and thigh as he spoke. "I would feel as if I were the only person in the world, as if everyone else had left without telling me. It was the emptiest, loneliest feeling."

He looked down at her, his dark eyes reflecting the fire, burning into her soul. "I haven't felt like that since the first time I kissed you. That time by the lake."

There were tears in her eyes as she pulled him closer to her. With her body, with her heart, she began to banish the terrible memory from his mind.

Eight

Abby's eyelids weighed a ton. She raised them slowly and with what seemed like a great effort. For a long, disoriented moment she concentrated sleepily on the hard lump under her back, the strange musty odor in the air, and the dust floating in the stream of bright sunlight that slid through a large crack in the wall . . .

Crack in the wall? Suddenly she was wide awake. She tried to sit up, but before she could move, an arm was extended across her chest, pushing her back to the mattress. Jerking her gaze to the right, she stared at Joe, who lay beside her with his eyes still closed.

"Don't move," he whispered.

Abby froze, her mind flooding with visions of rattlesnakes at her feet, curled and ready to strike. "Why?" she whispered anxiously.

He sat up and leaned over her. "Because I haven't kissed you yet."

Exhaling the breath she had been holding, she glared at him. "One of these days," she muttered threateningly.

"No, now," he corrected softly, then his lips

found hers. After a particularly satisfying kiss, he spoke again, his voice low and lazy. "I watched you while you slept last night. You kept smiling in your sleep."

The smile she gave him was pure sensuality. "I must have been having another one of *those* dreams."

"That's it," he said suddenly. "That's the smile." He raised one heavy brow and the scar on his forehead seemed to dip lower. "What are *those* dreams about?"

With one finger she leisurely outlined his lips. "Oh . . . this and that. Maybe a little more of this than of that."

Pushing on his shoulders, she moved until she was leaning over him. Her golden brown hair fell to either side of his face as she studied his features, memorizing every bone, every wrinkle. She ran a finger over the uneven line of his nose and the squareness of his strong jaw.

"Didn't I mention that I've been having a lot of X-rated dreams lately?" she asked softly.

Now both heavy brows rose in a silent, sensual comment. "Ver-ry inter-resting," he murmured in a parody of a heavy German accent. "So tell me, my dear young lady, how long have you been having these so erotic dreams? We must discover whether you have the classic father fixation or are merely obsessed with feather pillows."

"My pillows are foam rubber."

He clasped his hand to his brow in astonishment. "A foam rubber fixation? Mein Gott! I believe we are breaking new ground here."

She laughed softly, moving her body slowly against his. "Do you think I could possibly have a

Joe fixation? You see, Herr Doctor," she whispered huskily, "I've had them since the first time you kissed me."

He sucked in a sharp breath and reached up to pull her to him, his grasp painfully urgent. After the first intense moment, his grip eased and the kiss mellowed. Then slowly the enchantment began again and wheels of colored fire turned for them both.

Even after his heart slowed its hectic pace and his breathing returned to normal, Joe still held her. He didn't want to let go of her. He held her tightly to him, stroking her hair with rough, shaky caresses as another kind of urgency took hold of him.

"I don't want to leave," he whispered harshly. "I want to keep you prisoner in this broken-down cabin forever."

"I know, I know," she agreed softly, kissing his hand as it passed her lips. "I want that too." She sighed. "But I'm afraid we have to get back to reality."

He closed his eyes tightly, then, as though something had exploded inside him, he gripped her shoulders and stared at her fiercely. "Dammit, Abby, this *is* reality!" he said in a rough, strained voice. He took her hand and pressed it to his groin where he was now so vulnerable. "Feel me. I'm real. I'm not 'pulsing with desire' and I'm still holding you; I still want you."

He stared into her startled eyes and said, "You said you would feel guilty about a casual affair. Do you feel guilty?" He gave her a small shake. "Do you?"

She shook her head, her disheveled hair swirling around her face.

"Of course you don't. What we have together is not strawberry-flavored douche and a diaphragm shoved into your purse at the last minute." He lifted her hand to his heart, his grip hurting. "It's beating, Abby; *that* is reality." He held both her hands to his lips and kissed each palm hungrily.

"You're in me here and here and here," he said as he pressed her right hand to his groin, then his heart, and then his head. His voice was quiet but heartstoppingly intense when he said, "Open your eyes and *see* me. Please, Abby," he whispered. "Let me in."

Abby stared at him in confusion and pain. She had hurt him in some way, hurt him terribly. But she couldn't understand how. And she didn't know what to do to make it right.

"Joe," she whispered. Her mouth was so dry, the word was almost painful. "I'm sorry. I didn't mean—"

"Wait," he said, interrupting her jerkily. He sucked in a raspy breath and closed his eyes tightly. When he opened them again, his eyes were strangely sad. "Never mind, sweetheart," he whispered. Then almost to himself he added, "It was too soon, too damn soon."

"Joe, tell me . . . *please.*"

He hugged her hard, then held her away from him to give her a smile that made her dizzy. It was as though the world had decided to start spinning again.

"Not now," he said, gracefully standing up. "I

promise you we'll talk later, but right now I think we had better try to find our way back to the car before Bardle sends out a search party."

"Sweet heaven," she breathed anxiously, his reminder wiping everything else temporarily from her mind. "I forgot all about them."

His laugh told her he was pleased with her statement. "Well, I don't think they've forgotten about you."

They were dressed within minutes and hurriedly left the cabin with Merry trailing behind on his leash. After searching the area for a while, Joe found ruts where an old road had once led to the cabin. It was heavily overgrown and would have been impossible to see in the dim light of the night before, but now it was clearly visible.

"I only hope the car is still there," Joe said, wrapping his arm around Abby as they followed the trail. He glanced at Merry, who stopped every few minutes to investigate bushes and clumps of weeds. "If I had known he was going to go hunting for the gingerbread house, I'd have taken the keys out of the car . . . or at least dropped a few crumbs. We may have to walk back to Canton to get help."

But they were lucky. When they reached the blacktop road at last, they found his Buick just as they had left it the night before. Within minutes they were once more on their way to Bardle.

As they drew nearer to Abby's hometown, she began to worry about the consequences of their adventure. It was still early, she reasoned. Maybe no one knew she and Joe hadn't returned home last night.

After saying a hasty good-bye and distractedly acknowledging his promise to call, Abby stepped cautiously from Joe's car. She didn't see a soul as she and Merry walked through the front gate. And not a single curtain fluttered as she let herself into the house. She said a small prayer of thanksgiving. Maybe no one had noticed.

Five minutes after she'd opened her front door, the phone began to ring.

Joe's steps slowed as he climbed Abby's porch. He grinned when he pictured her reaction to what was happening in her Bardle. *I probably won't find it so amusing when she starts to blast me*, he thought, shaking his head.

He opened the screen door and raised his hand to knock, but before his knuckles could even touch the wood, the door was opened just a crack. Then suddenly a slender arm snaked out, grasped him roughly by the collar, and hauled him urgently inside.

"Joe," Abby said, her voice panicky as she parted the curtains a bit to look out at the street. "They all know, Joe." The words came out in a frantic whisper. "Everyone in town knows we didn't come home last night."

He didn't respond. Anything he had to say now would be lost in her panic. He couldn't, however, keep a brief smile from playing across his lips as he watched her.

She closed her eyes for a second, then opened them wide to stare at him in horror. "And that's not all. They're *thrilled*, Joe." Her hand moved to grasp his arm tightly. "Do you understand what that means? Do you know why they're all so pleased?"

"Abby, Abby," he said, pulling her against him, hoping she wouldn't notice that his body was rocking with laughter. "Calm down, babe. It's not that bad."

She jerked her head up to stare at him incredulously. "Not that bad! Joe, listen carefully." Her eyelids closed as she said the next words slowly. "They're asking if we've set the wedding date."

He nodded. "Yes, I know."

Moaning miserably, she buried her face in his chest and her words were muffled in his shirt. "You mean they've been asking you too?"

"Uh-huh," he said agreeably.

"What did you tell them?" She glanced up at him again. "I didn't know what to say. No words, no excuses, would come out of my mouth. I simply ran and hid."

He smiled down at her and as the silence continued she suddenly became very still. "Joe," she said warily, "what did you tell them?"

"I told them I want the kids to get to know me first so it would probably be several months before we got married," he said calmly.

"You *what*!"

He flinched as the anticipated explosion came with spectacular swiftness. "Now, babe," he said as he backed away from the fury in her eyes.

"Don't you 'now, babe' me," she hissed. "What were you thinking of? What in the world possessed you? This is carrying the joke a little too far. You'll go on your merry way after the school year and leave me holding the bag. Of all the addle-brained—"

She stopped to inhale deeply several times and muttered under her breath, "I'm calm. I'm calm."

Then she stared up at him and smiled stiffly. "I'm calm now, Joe," she said sweetly. "Would you mind telling me why you did such an *asinine* thing? That is, if you don't mind," she added considerately.

"It isn't a joke. I meant it."

She reacted to his softly spoken words as though he had dropped a bomb, her eyes reflecting her shock.

"Ever since I met you, you've been trying to keep me out of the mainstream of your life," he continued. "It won't work, Abby. I'm in it and I'm going to stay in it."

She shook her head vigorously. "You don't know what you're saying. Joe, you can't possibly—"

"I do know and I can possibly." He clasped her neck with both hands, lifting her chin until she met his eyes. "Abby, I love you. Will you marry me?" He ran his large, rough thumb across her lips. "You're sunshine, Abby. And through you, the world shines for me. For the first time in my life I feel like a whole person. You did that, Abby. In two months you've given me more than I ever dreamed was possible for me. You make me real." His voice dropped to a low, husky whisper. "Say yes, Abby."

Abby closed her eyes and the words rippled through her as though they were physically penetrating every inch of her body. He loved her. He wanted to marry her.

A blinding light exploded in her head, a light that was love, that she could feel filling the room. She could feel it in him, in herself. It was a miracle in an age when miracles weren't supposed to happen.

For a delicious few seconds she ignored every question, every objection, and simply let the joy permeate her flesh.

But the objections wouldn't stay contained for very long and eventually she opened her eyes. Staring up at him, she whispered, "Oh, Joe, I've never in my life had anything so beautiful happen to me. But—"

"No buts, Abby," he said softly. "Just say yes."

She shook her head slightly. "Don't you see? You wouldn't simply be marrying me. You would be taking on a whole family. You don't even know Brennie and Jeff."

"I know Jeff," he corrected. "We got to know each other very well on the camping trip. And I'm sure it will be just as easy to get to know Brennie."

"Easy?" she said, raking her fingers through her hair as she walked a couple of steps away from him. "Nothing is ever easy where kids are concerned. And you got to know Jeff as a football hero, not as a father. Believe me, that's a completely different thing." She shook her head. "The first time you tell him he can't blow up the attic, your superstar status will slip immeasurably."

"And it should." He stared at her for a moment. "Don't you think I can succeed as a father without a big name to back me up?"

She had hurt him again. Without thinking, without meaning to, she had hurt him badly. She could see it in his eyes, even though his expression was guarded. In some way they were already tied to each other and his pain ripped at her.

Walking back to him, she slipped her arms around his waist and leaned her head against his chest. "I'm sorry," she whispered. "I didn't mean that the way it sounded. I think you would be a success at anything you set your mind to. I simply wanted you to know what you're trying to take on." As she reached up to touch his face, some of the hurt seemed to fade. "Are you sure you want to try?"

"I'm sure. But Abby"—he held her chin in one large hand, his thumb stroking her cheek in a strangely intense caress—"are you willing to give me a chance? Can you hold back the doubts long enough for us to see if it will work?"

He didn't know what he was asking of her, she thought. How could she hold back the doubts when she knew what was ahead of them and he didn't? She had no doubt that Brennie and Jeff would accept Joe, but could Joe accept all the problems that went along with acquiring a ready-made family?

She drew a deep breath. The questions would never be answered until they gave it a try. And if anyone was worth taking a chance on, she knew, it was Joe. "Okay, quarterback," she said, grinning. "I'm game if you are. What do we do first?"

His arms around her tightened painfully as he drew a harsh, shaky breath. Then he began to laugh, whirling her around in a joyous circle. "First we go get the kids," he said, his eyes burning with excitement. "If they're going to get to know me, we might as well start now."

Before Abby could catch her breath, they were in Joe's Buick headed toward her parents' house. She chewed thoughtfully on her fingernail, then turned to glance at him. "You know, it's probably a good thing we're going to pick the kids up now. The way gossip spreads around here, my parents may already have dropped subtle hints to Brennie and Jeff about having a new father."

"Will you mind?" he asked, glancing at her sharply. "If they already know?"

"No," she said slowly. "They'll know sooner or later, but I'd like it to come from us."

He nodded, then gave a short laugh. "I never thought I'd be terrified of two kids. What if they hate the idea?"

"They won't," she said, giving his hard thigh a reassuring squeeze. "They're normal kids. They give love freely to anyone who wants it." She grinned at him. "I don't want to brag, but I have a couple of pretty smart kids. They'll see right away that you're someone special."

Giving her a doubtful look, he said, "Maybe we should wait a little while to tell them . . . just until they get to know me better."

Abby hid her relief in a brilliant smile. "That would probably be best. It would give you all a chance to relax and learn about each other."

After a moment of thoughtful silence, he asked, "What about your mother and father? What do you think they'll say about all this?"

Abby shook her head. "I don't know. They want me to be happy, and I know my mother thinks a woman is nothing without a man to guide her and provide for her."

"Your mother sounds like an extremely intelligent woman," he said, grinning.

"You would think so, wouldn't you?" she teased, laughing. "Which shows how much you know about it. I don't need anyone to provide for me, and I saw what kind of guide you were last night in the woods."

"I think I did very well. I got us just exactly where I wanted us to be." He gave her a look that made the very air sizzle, then laughed in delight when she muttered, "Stop that!"

"What about your father?" he asked after a moment. "What will he think about it?"

She shrugged. "Dad's pretty cautious. He trusts me, but he may reserve judgment until he knows you better." She sighed. "I may be getting ahead of things. They may not know a thing about it."

But as soon as they pulled up in the driveway of her parents' house to the accompaniment of three barking dogs, Abby knew her parents had definitely heard the gossip.

In any other circumstances Abby would have spent her usual few minutes admiring her parents' home. The old-fashioned frame house was topped by a green, high-peaked roof, and a trellis covered with morning glories closed in one side of the large porch.

This was not the home of her childhood. During Abby's growing-up years they had lived in Bardle, near her father's small grocery store. It was only after Abby had married that her father decided to return to his roots and buy the small farm they were now so proud of.

And Abby was proud for them. Ordinarily, when she visited them, she saw the fulfillment of her parents' dream as a positive statement of life's possibilities.

But today was not ordinary and Abby didn't see the things she usually noticed. Her attention was caught and held by the two people standing on the porch. Her father's bushy eyebrows couldn't have gone any higher on his forehead without merging with his gray hair and her mother looked as if she was about to burst.

Luckily, though, they hadn't said anything to Jeff and Brennie. There was no awkwardness in the way the children greeted Abby and Joe. Abby took a backseat and merely watched as Joe proceeded to charm her children and her parents. There was no hesitancy in his manner now. An unbiased observer couldn't possibly have known he was nervous, she decided.

After the introductions had been taken care of, Brennie and Jeff, with only the mildest of protests, went to pack their bags. For a few seconds the four people in the living room simply sat and looked at each other.

"So Joe," her father said gruffly, "how do you think you'll like coaching at a small-town high school?"

The only sign that Joe recognized the question as the beginning of an interrogation was the way his fingers plucked at the fabric of the chair on which he sat. Abby hid her grin, wondering if he felt as much like a teenager as she did.

Joe cleared his throat. "Well, sir, I think coaching is coaching wherever you happen to do it. I'm enjoying the easygoing atmosphere of Texas, but when it comes down to getting on with the game, I don't think it'll matter where the boys come from."

Her father nodded solemnly. "And do you have any plans for after the school year?"

"I beg your pardon?"

Abby couldn't hold back her amusement any longer. She burst out laughing, rising to move quickly across the room. She sat down on the arm of her father's chair, leaning down to kiss his lined forehead. "I think what Dad's asking you, Joe, is if you think you can support me in the manner to which I've become accustomed."

"Abby!" her father said, his tone scolding. "Nobody said anything like that."

"I know, but it's pretty clear that you two have heard something about Joe and me," she pointed out. She smiled at them lovingly. "You don't have to beat around the bush with us. Joe and I have decided to get married."

She smiled at her mother's excited, "Oh, Abby," then continued. "We aren't going to tell the kids yet because we want them to get to know Joe first."

Joe's eyes went from Abby's mother to her father. "I know this must seem a little sudden to you, but I . . . well, I hope you'll be happy for us."

"We just want Abby to be happy," Sally said, smiling.

Joe glanced at John. "Mr. Holcomb?"

Her father was silent for a moment as he looked up at his daughter. "Her life will be different," he said slowly. "You're a wealthy man and a celebrity." He paused, then looked Joe straight in the eyes. "Just try not to take her too far away from us."

Joe inhaled deeply, then smiled. "I don't think you're talking about physical distances, sir, and believe me, Abby knows who she is. I wouldn't ever try to change that."

Her father stood up. "I think you'd better start calling me John. Now why don't we have some of that peach brandy Sally saves for her canasta club?"

When Brennie and Jeff reentered the living room, they paid no attention to the celebration going on. Brennie wanted her mother to see the dress her grandmother had made for her and Jeff pulled steadily on Joe's arm, fervently urging him outside to view his pig.

Joe allowed himself to be led out of the house, shrugging as he glanced over his shoulder at Abby. The pigpen was a comfortable distance from the house, situated out of sight behind a small stand of trees.

Standing on the bottom rung of the high fence of the pen, Joe gazed down at the animal that was, in its own way, strangely attractive. "That's a pig, all right," he said with an admiring grin.

"Best of the litter, Pop says," Jeff bragged.

"Where's Brennie's pig?" Joe asked, glancing at the other animals.

Jeff didn't answer right away. He stared off into the distance at a tree-topped hill. "She died," he said finally, then hopped down from the fence and moved to sit under a chinaberry tree several yards away.

"I'm sorry about that, Jeff," Joe said quietly. Following the boy, he eased his large frame down beside him. "Was Brennie very upset?"

He nodded. "At first she was, but Mom talked to her on the phone and she stopped crying." He gazed up at Joe. "I think it reminded her of Daddy dying."

"How about you?" he probed gently. "Did it remind you of that too?"

Jeff leaned his head back against the smooth

bark of the tree. "Yeah, I guess it did." He turned solemn eyes toward Joe. "Why does it happen, Joe? Why do things die?"

Joe felt his heart begin to beat faster. What could he say? he wondered. How on earth could he answer a question like that? Was this what parenting was all about? Doing the impossible?

"That's a tough one, Jeff," he said slowly, knowing that platitudes were not what the boy needed to hear. "I suppose someone has already told you that thing about God needing your Dad up in heaven?"

Jeff nodded. "Harry's mother said that. I didn't believe it though. It doesn't make sense. I mean, God can do anything he wants to. How can he need my Dad more than I do?"

"I agree. It doesn't make sense." He hesitated, hoping against hope that he wouldn't fail Jeff. "Jeff, I'm going to give you one of the secrets of being grown-up. Do you think you can handle it?"

The boy thought for a second. "I guess so. Mom says she tells me everything because I only absorb the stuff I can use. So I guess if I can't handle it, I'll just forget it."

Joe looked down at the young face and spoke quietly. "When you get to be an adult, Jeff, you find out that there simply are no answers to the most important questions. At least not answers that we can understand. I could tell you there was some grand and mysterious reason why your father died, but the plain truth is I just don't know. That's what you learn and come to accept when you grow up. You learn that you'll never have all the answers."

Jeff stared at the ground, poking at the brown

earth with a stick. After a while he leaned his head back and stared at the blue sky in silence, his young, thin face uncharacteristically still.

Had he done the right thing? Joe asked himself later, as he and Jeff walked back to the house. Should he have told him to talk to Abby about it?

He sighed heavily. No, he couldn't have done that. Jeff had asked him an honest question and he had expected an honest answer. Joe had given him the truth, but the truth wasn't very satisfying sometimes.

He couldn't help feeling that he had failed miserably in his first attempt to establish a sound relationship with Abby's children. What did he know about being a parent, anyway? Kids were so sensitive. What if he did something out of ignorance that screwed them up for life?

Glancing up, he saw Brennie running toward them and forced the doubts out of his mind. What he was facing was the toughest challenge of his life, he knew, but he had more to gain than ever before, and he couldn't let himself give up before he had tried his damnedest.

At the kitchen window, Abby held back the white lace curtain and watched Joe walk back to the house. Brennie held his hand while Jeff walked backwards in front of them, talking his normal ninety miles a minute. The three of them made a picture that would stay with her forever, a picture that made her heart ache with pleasure.

As they drew nearer, she noticed something new in Joe's face, a sadness about the eyes, an uneasiness that hadn't been there a few minutes before. What had happened out there with her son? Surely it wasn't possible that Joe was having second thoughts already?

"They look good together," her mother said from directly behind her. Sally walked to the much-used wooden table and sat down, picking up the bowl of black-eyed peas that she was snapping for their dinner. "He must be a special man," she added quietly.

Abby walked quickly to where her mother sat and knelt beside her, taking her hands in hers to hold them tight. "Mama," she said huskily, "he thinks *I'm* special."

"And so he should," her mother said, nodding. "You *are* special."

Abby laughed, a small laugh that caught in her throat. "I'm not. I'm not special at all. I'm just . . . just ordinary." She closed her eyes tightly, laying her head in her mother's lap. "I'm so scared, Mama. I've never felt so loved before and I'm afraid it won't last. He's everything I've ever wanted in a man."

She opened her eyes to look up at her mother. "I wouldn't even admit to myself that I loved him until he asked me to marry him. But I do, more than anything in the world. Mama," she whispered, "he said I make him real. What if I can't live up to that?"

Sally began to stroke her daughter's hair gently. "You stop that kind of talk right now, Abigail. Haven't I always told you that you do what you have to do? That's what living is all about. And if he thinks you're special, then by heaven, Abby, you'll be special."

"But how?" she asked, standing up and pacing in front of her mother in agitation. After a moment she stopped to pick up one of the long green pods, twisting it until it snapped. "Where do you buy a book that teaches you how to be special?"

"You just be yourself. Who do you think he sees when he looks at you? Do you think he sees Queen Elizabeth?" Sally snorted indelicately. "No, he sees Abigail Fisher and that's who he wants."

"I wish—" Abby began, then broke off as Joe stepped into the room.

When his gaze found her, an unbelievable light came into his eyes. At that moment she knew her mother was right. She would do anything for this man, and if he thought she was special, then by heaven, she would be special.

Nine

The next week was a week of peace for Abby and Joe. The time for the annual old pioneers reunion had arrived and everyone in Bardle was involved in the feverish preparations. It was a carnival, country fair, and town reunion all rolled up in one gigantic festival. Baking contests and beauty contests, fiddle contests and dancing contests. Prizes given to the oldest settler in Dannen County and to the couple who had been married for the shortest length of time. All this and more were part of the general festivities.

Abby desperately needed the time of peace. She needed to be able to relax with Joe. He spent every daylight hour with the three of them, and she could see that already the kids were coming to depend on him.

Three weeks after their trip to Canton, at the height of the reunion, Joe arrived at Abby's house to find chaos reigning. When Abby met him at the door, there was a harried look on her face.

Giving him a quick kiss of greeting, she called over her shoulder, "Brennie, go into Jeff's room and see if you can find his dark blue pants."

"*Mo*-ther!" Brennie squealed. "I can't go in there. I simply can't."

Abby rolled her eyes in exasperation and started to walk away, but Joe caught her hand and swiftly pulled her back into his arms. "*Mo*-ther," he mimicked softly. "Why can't she go in there?"

Abby looked up at him and sighed. "Have you ever seen Jeff's room? It's like no-man's land." She shook her head. "I swear there are pockets of Japanese in there who haven't heard that the war is over."

Laughing quietly, he made her lean against him while he rubbed the taut tendons in her neck. "Do you want to tell me what the crisis is this time? I thought I heard you tell Jeff last night that he could wear his light blue slacks for the fiddle contest."

She nodded wearily, moaning when his fingers found a particularly painful spot. "I did. But Jeff decided to chase Merry through Eb's rose-bushes and that was the end of the light blue pants."

Joe inhaled the scent that belonged only to Abby. It had been so long since he had been alone with her, so long since they had made love. Too long. Her soft flesh felt so good against him. He could still see the way she'd looked with the flickering firelight touching her body—the most beautiful woman he had ever seen. The memory of her filled his dreams night after night.

His hand roamed down her back, finding the sensitive spot at the base of her spine.

"Joe," she whispered huskily, lifting her head to stare at him with sensually dazed eyes. Then she echoed his thoughts. "It's been so long. I don't know if I can manage to hold out for another month."

"I know," he said, his voice hoarse. "Believe me, *I know*. But we agreed we needed to give Brennie and Jeff a chance to adjust."

She nodded and the regret in her eyes filled him with an aching desire. "At least you can kiss me properly," she said, her lower lip drooping in a sexy pout. "We may not get another chance tonight."

He lowered his head, his breath coming faster in anticipation. Her lips were only a fraction of an inch away.

"Mother!" Brennie's shriek would have pierced the eardrums of anyone standing within ten feet of her. A second later she appeared in the doorway, her beautiful brown hair hanging in disheveled hanks around her face and a disgusted look on her young face. "Mother, he has food under his bed and it's . . . it's *growing*!"

Abby looked down at her watch and the harried look returned to her eyes. She glanced at Brennie, then over her daughter's shoulder toward Jeff's room. Suddenly she shoved the hairbrush she was carrying into Joe's hand and said, "Here, fix her hair. And if I'm not out in three days, call the State Troopers."

Joe looked blankly at the hairbrush, then at Brennie, who was watching him expectantly. He couldn't help thinking that this was some kind of test. Mentally crossing his fingers, he gave her his most self-assured smile.

"Okay, Brennie. It looks like I'm going to be in charge of that beautiful hair of yours. Come put yourself in the hands of the master."

She giggled and settled on the floor in front of the leather recliner, which he assumed he was supposed to occupy. Stepping over her, he sat on the edge of the chair and started to brush her hair.

"You usually wear it in braids, don't you?"

She nodded. "Except to church. Mom lets me wear it down on Sunday. She says it's because she wants the Lord to see how pretty it is, but it's really because she never has time to braid it on Sunday morning."

He drew a bracing breath. "Well, since this is Saturday, I guess it will have to be braids."

Fifteen minutes later he turned Brennie around and leaned back to observe the finished product. After a moment he said slowly, "Brennie, is one of them supposed to be shorter than the other one?"

Jumping up, she walked to the oval mirror that decorated the wall above a walnut table. She burst out laughing when she saw her reflection. Tilting her head so that the braids hung evenly, she said, "It looks like my head is on crooked." She glanced back at him. "You're so funny, Joe."

He grinned halfheartedly. "I thought you'd appreciate it. Now I think we'd better stop fooling around and get it fixed right."

When she was seated, he reached out to undo the unconventional braids and begin the process again.

After another fifteen minutes Joe began to feel that tackling the entire Dallas Cowboy football team would have been an easier task than what he was attempting now. After securing the last braid, he laid down the brush with a frustrated sigh and said, "Brennie, you know that new rock group who wear off-center braids?"

Her nod was doubtful to say the least, but he didn't require a lot of encouragement.

"Have you ever considered copying their hairstyle?" he asked in a low, devious voice.

The sound of Brennie's laughter reached Abby as she finally located Jeff's pants in his toybox. Thanking the Lord for polyester, she threw them across the room to him.

Brennie had begun to look forward to Joe's visits as much as Jeff did, but Abby wondered how she would react to having him for a father. She knew that sooner or later they would have to tell the kids, but Abby wanted to make sure Joe could cope with what he was getting into before they made the announcement.

Giving Jeff strict orders not to move an inch from his bedroom until they left the house, Abby passed Brennie in the hall and her eyes widened when she saw her daughter's hair. "Brennie—" she sputtered.

Brennie swung around, giving Abby a full view of the ponytail that was pulled provocatively to one side of her head. "Don't you love it?" she asked, smiling dreamily. "Joe said it made me look fourteen at least."

"At least," Abby muttered under her breath, and left her daughter to go and seek out the perpetrator.

In the living room she found Joe whistling casually under his breath, but eyeing her warily. She laughed at his guilty expression and said, "What happened to the braids? She looks like Lolita."

Heaving a sigh of relief, he said, "Honest, Abby, I tried, but something always went wrong. One was either too high or too close to the back of her head." He shook his head. "She thought I was doing it on purpose."

She raised an arched brow as she walked to the living room closet. "And you're still alive to tell me about it? If I get so much as one hair out of place, she acts like she's ruined for life." Reaching up to pull something from the shelf, she added, "I only hope she doesn't expect to wear it like that all the time."

Turning around to face him, she held out a violin that had seen better days. "This is a fiddle," she said in her best teacher's voice. "I can tell you're thinking, 'Of course, that's a fiddle,' but I want you to examine it very carefully because when Jeff starts to play tonight, I don't want to hear you say, 'What *is* that?' "

He chuckled. "Is he that bad?"

"I'm afraid so," she said, grinning. "But he enjoys it and that's what counts." She glanced around the room, wondering if she was forgetting anything. "I guess we're ready."

"You sound surprised."

"I am. I can't remember the last time we were actually early for anything." She smiled at him. "You must be a good influence."

She shouted for Brennie and Jeff, and five minutes later they had piled into Joe's Buick and were on their way to the old city park that had been the location of the pioneers reunion since it was first held.

Before they reached the park, Abby turned around in her seat and caught Jeff's eye. "Jeff, this time when you get to the "Orangeblossom Special," I think it would be better if you didn't try doing the Moonwalk."

"But Mom," he protested over Brennie's giggle, "it's my best thing."

"Stop laughing, Brennie. I know it is, Jeff, and it shows a lot of ingenuity and . . . and panache. But not more than two people in the audience will even have heard of break dancing or seen Michael Jackson do it."

Joe glanced over his shoulder at Jeff and Abby saw him give her son a sympathetic shrug.

"And besides," Brennie added smugly, "you can't look behind you with the violin under your chin and you always trip over something."

"Oh, all right," Jeff said in resignation. "Then I guess I'd better take off the glove." He pulled his right hand from behind his back and took off one of Abby's bright orange gardening gloves.

Abby could see Joe's shoulders shaking with laughter and she had a difficult time keeping her face straight, especially when he whispered, "The Moonwalk with the "Orangeblossom Special"? I'm sorry I'll have to miss that."

They found seats in the second row in front of the makeshift wooden stage and sat down to wait for Jeff's turn in front of the microphone. It was stifling hot and Joe looked around to see painted paper fans being waved leisurely by several people in the audience.

"I've only seen that kind of fan in museums," he whispered to Abby. "Along with Wilkie campaign buttons and Dr. Abercrombie's All-Purpose Panacea. I thought they were extinct."

"Maybe in Brooklyn they're extinct, but in

Bardle they're alive and well," Abby said indignantly. "They're the feedstore's only form of advertisement."

Joe turned back to the stage as the first boy in Jeff's category was announced. Although of the same age, the boy who walked up to the microphone was taller and heavier than Jeff. He played very well for his age and never once during his performance did he smile, but merely stared solemnly at a point well above the audience's heads.

After the third boy had played and after he had listened to three variations of the "Orangeblossom Special," Joe decided that Jeff had some pretty stiff competition. Apparently the youth of this area took their fiddling seriously, he thought.

Then Jeff stepped up to the microphone, a grin of pure joy spreading across his thin face. Joe looked around at the audience to see if they were as affected by the boy's exuberance as he was. Sure enough, he found echoing grins on many faces.

When he began to play, Jeff played with his entire body. Every part of him seemed to be keeping time with the lively music. Joe supposed Jeff's playing wasn't technically as good as that of the other contestants, but he felt a curious swelling of pride in his chest as he watched Jeff put his whole heart and soul into the music.

When the tempo of the music changed and Jeff swung into the "Orangeblossom Special," Joe could almost feel the boy itching to perform the graceful, backward sliding steps of the Moonwalk and he turned to find Abby sharing his laughter.

Even without the controversial choreography, Jeff's performance was apparently a hit. What he lacked in expertise, he made up for in enthusiasm, and the applause rang out under the canvas canopy.

And even though he didn't win the competition, Jeff was satisfied just to have participated. When the award had been presented and Jeff had been pounded on the back by a dozen different people, he began to pull them toward the carnival grounds, toward the smell of cotton candy and popcorn, toward the sound of loud, mechanical music—a weird blend of Brahms and the Beatles.

Jeff and Brennie immediately made for the wilder rides, but when Abby sent a questioning glance toward Joe, he shook his head vehemently. Abby let out a sigh of relief and led him toward the more familiar Ferris wheel.

"Does this mean we're getting old?" Abby asked laughingly as they slowly rode to the top of the giant wheel.

"No," he said emphatically. "It simply means we're more reluctant to lose the contents of our stomachs."

"Well, that sounds better anyway." She leaned over to wave to a group of people, then said, "Uh-oh. I think Brennie's new hairstyle is a hit."

Joe looked down to see Brennie shyly talking to a boy with slicked-back hair, black leather wrist-guards, and what looked like a tow chain wrapped around his neck.

"Abby," he said in alarm, twisting in the seat as the Ferris wheel passed the observation point. "What's she doing with him? He looks like he's out of prison on a weekend pass."

Abby laughed at his expression, feeling a deep pleasure spread through her. "Calm down. What you're experiencing now is called 'The Papa Syndrome.' It happens to all fathers."

"But aren't you worried?" he asked, craning his neck to try and spot the young couple. "He looks like a hood."

"That hood is Jimmy Bob Summers. He puts on a disguise during the week and fools people into thinking he's merely a bag boy at the Piggly-Wiggly."

Joe stared at her in surprise. "That's the nice-looking kid who carries my groceries to the car?"

She nodded. "The same. His father is the local insurance man and a very good friend of Harrison's. You've probably met him."

He shook his head in bewilderment. "But why is he dressed like that?"

"This is only a guess, you understand," she said, her expression too solemn. He could tell she was having trouble keeping a straight face. "But I would say it's to impress cute young girls like Brennie."

"How can she be impressed?" he asked, giving her a disgruntled look. "He looks like he bought his clothes at an auto parts store."

Abby patted his knee soothingly. "To you and me maybe, but to Brennie he probably looks like a knight on a white charger."

The rueful way he shook his head made Abby laugh again. Oh, how she loved this man, she thought. More and more each day. She realized now that she had never felt really complete until he'd come into her life and forcefully showed her that she couldn't do without him.

"Are you still worried about Brennie?" she asked after a moment.

"Actually I wasn't thinking of Brennie at all."

The sensual twist of his lower lip caused her pulse rate to skyrocket. She couldn't take her eyes off his face as she asked, "Just exactly what *are* you thinking about?"

"I was just wondering how difficult it would be to make love to you in a Ferris wheel car." He smiled. "And I was thinking that it wouldn't matter how difficult it was if there weren't a thousand people down there who could see us."

She moved closer, aching to feel more of his warmth, and stared straight ahead. "I like the way your mind works," she said softly. "In fact, I'm fond of the way a lot of things about you work."

He had his arm around her shoulders and now one hand slid under her arm to press against a rounded breast. "Lady, you sure do pick strange places to get provocative," he said in a husky whisper.

Their eyes met and held, each of them recognizing the hunger visible in the other's expression. Joe lowered his head slowly, his eyes never leaving her face, and only when he was a whisper away did her eyelids drift shut. A delicious lethargy took hold of her.

When she felt the touch of his mouth, she moved her lips lazily against his, trying to memorize the dizzying sensation. The kiss was slow and drugging and carried her away from reality on a dream. It was only when he began to move more urgently against her that she finally found the strength to lift her hand to touch him.

And just as her hand met the warm flesh of his neck, the sound of applause burst in on them. Blinking swiftly, Abby looked up to find that their car on the ferris wheel had stopped at ground level and that half of Bardle had seen their kiss.

She tried desperately to sink into the seat, but Joe wouldn't allow it. Urging her to stand, he held her hand tightly as he made a sweeping bow; there was nothing left for her to do but curtsy.

"Joe Gilbraithe," she said as they walked from the laughing crowd at the Ferris wheel, "you couldn't be satisfied with disgracing me once, could you? You had to try for an encore."

"I beg your pardon?" he said, giving her an injured look. "Was I the one who chased Merry into the woods? And was I the one who got provocative so far above sea level?"

"Those are technicalities," she said, airily waving aside his objections. "If I hadn't been with *you*, neither of those things would have happened."

He laughed warmly at her response. "You use very strange logic, Abby. And to make it up to me, you have to win me a stuffed elephant."

Abby glanced at the booth they were passing. It was a miniature rifle range with ducks floating and bears marching to the sound of "Stars and Stripes Forever." "You don't think I can do it, do you?" she asked, her eyes brightening at the challenge. Joe only smiled.

Moving to the counter, she laid down her quarter and picked up one of the rifles. Three minutes later Joe walked away from the booth carrying a small purple elephant.

"Remind me never to make you mad," he said as he studied her warily from the corners of his eyes.

She laughed. "I was on the rifle team in high

school," she confessed. "I know it was cheating, but I simply couldn't resist." Glancing down at her watch, she said, "We had better round up Brennie and Jeff now or I'll never get them up for church tomorrow."

It took a little doing to convince Jeff that he didn't have to ride everything in the carnival "one more time," but eventually they got the kids home and into bed.

The harsh heat of the long day had faded into a warm, velvety night when Abby and Joe walked into the backyard. For a while they strolled slowly, inhaling the scent of Eb's roses. Then Joe pulled her down on the chaise lounge and leaned back with her in his arms, her back against his chest.

Wrapping his arms around her, he crossed his hands on her stomach. "It's funny," he said in a soft whisper, unwilling to disturb the tranquillity of the night.

"What's funny?" she asked lazily. Her head lay against his shoulder as she stared at the brilliant canopy of stars above them.

"Everything. Holding you like this."

She turned her head to give him an inquiring glance. "You find this funny?"

"I find it strange," he said, smiling down at her. "I've never been so frustrated in my life, but on the other hand I've never been so satisfied, so full."

"I know." She laid her hands on his and pressed them closer, returning her head to its comfortable position on his chest. "I feel the same way. It's as though I finally know what life's all about."

He leaned his head down to rub it against her hair. "The only thing that could possibly make it more complete would be being able to get up off this lounge chair and walk with you to our bedroom."

Turning her head slightly, she met his lips on the descent. The kiss was a promise for the future, and she turned her body into it.

As his hands began to caress her back, they heard a voice floating across the yard. Joe pulled his head back to stare at the house next door for a moment; then he said, "Yes, Mrs. Rappaport, I was just leaving."

"What did she say?" Abby asked as they stood and began to walk toward the gate leading out of the backyard.

When they reached the gate, Joe placed his hand on her neck and pulled her close for a short, rough kiss. "No one," he said, "but no one, questions Mrs. Rappaport." Then, with a sharp salute directed at Eb's house, he was gone.

Ten

The school year had begun at last. And one of the consequences was that Joe saw Abby even less than before. Abby was busy with her classes and with Brennie and Jeff. And Joe not only had the new experience of teaching to cope with, but also the fact that any free time he had was taken up by the football team.

He knew Abby had expected things to be more settled between them before the beginning of the school year, and twice she had talked to him about telling Brennie and Jeff of their wedding plans.

But both times Joe had stopped her. He knew she didn't understand what was behind his sudden hesitation, and somehow he simply couldn't bring himself to explain his feelings and his doubts to her.

As he walked down a school hall filled with early morning stillness, he thought of the weeks that had passed since he had proposed to Abby. During that time he had come to know and love her children. And he wanted more than ever for the four of them to be a real family. But two things stopped him from moving ahead with their plans.

The first was the fact that not once had Abby said she loved him. At times he could feel love for him pouring out of her. Then, in the dark of night, when he was away from the brilliance of her smile, the doubts would begin again. He just couldn't go ahead with their plans until he was absolutely sure of her feelings, he'd decided.

The other thing that stopped him was the doubt he felt about himself. Although he told himself he was creating problems, he still worried constantly about his ability to be the right kind of father to Brennie and Jeff. They were such special kids, he thought, and they deserved the best. But was he?

In the late evenings alone, he had tried reading books on parenting, but had found most of them confusing and contradictory. However, they did help him to recognize something very important. Raising children was a full-time job. A job that scared the hell out of him.

Brennie and Jeff seemed to like him well enough, but they still treated him like a friend of the family. How could he make them see him as a father instead? he wondered. He knew fatherhood had to be earned, but he simply didn't know how to go about it. When he had first thought of marrying Abby, he'd never dreamed that her children would be a problem. He loved them, didn't he? So what else did he have to know?

It was only when he was faced with the reality of having another human being depend on him that he saw how scary the job could be.

His steps slowed and his head began to ache when he thought of the possibility of losing Abby now that he had come to need her so much. He wanted her desperately, and the kids were a part of her. Whatever happened, he had to do right by the three of them.

Joe ran his hand roughly through his hair, then suddenly froze as he saw her walking toward him down the almost deserted hallway.

Abby's mind was not on where she was going. In fact, her mind wasn't on school at all. She was remembering, without a blush, the last time she and Joe had made love. Remembering the look and feel of him. Remembering the urgency of his hunger. Sweet heaven, it had been so long ago, she thought.

She saw him every day at school and every night at home, but almost never alone. At home Brennie and Jeff were always there, eager for Joe's attention. Then there were the friends who dropped by as regular as clockwork. And at school, even on his break, he was constantly surrounded by people.

Abby smiled suddenly. Along with everything else there was Joe's entourage. During the two weeks that school had been in session, he had somehow acquired an escort of three huge—and neckless—junior boys. They followed him everywhere. And so closely, she was afraid that if Joe ever stopped suddenly he would be trampled to death.

It seemed that they would never have time to themselves, time to talk and make love and establish a deep relationship. Sometimes when she looked at him, she saw something she didn't understand in his eyes. It worried her, and she wanted to find out what was bothering him. She wanted to—

She caught her breath in surprise when she saw him walking down the hall toward her . . . alone.

"Good morning, Evelyn," she murmured to the tall, thin woman who was just entering the empty classroom to Abby's right. "Good morning, Joe," Abby said, giving him a conspiratorial wink as she drew abreast of him.

"Good morning, Evelyn. Good morning, Abby." He waited silently until Evelyn, the Home Ec teacher, had closed her door, then glanced quickly over his shoulder to the left and to the right. When no one appeared in the hall, he grabbed Abby by the arm and pulled her through a door he'd quickly opened.

She stood in the dark, feeling his arms slide around her, and whispered, "Where are we?"

He chuckled softly and the sound vibrated warmly through her body. "In the broom closet. I rented it from the custodian. We've got it for the next ten minutes."

"Aren't we wasting rental time?" she suggested, and moved closer.

Seconds later the small room echoed with the increased tenor of their breathing. "Abby, Abby," he murmured huskily as he held her tightly. "I never get to hold you. I never get to kiss you."

"That's because we are simply never alone," she said, burying her face in his neck. "If it's not my friends at home, it's your Huey, Dewey, and Louie here at school. We shouldn't be so popular."

"It's you," he said. "People just naturally want to be around you." His hands traced her features in the dark as though trying to memorize each curve. "I may have to carry you away on my white stallion like the Sheikh of Araby. We could live alone in the desert . . . just you"—he kissed her forehead— "and me"—he kissed her nose—"and the five hundred women in my harem." He tried to kiss her lips, but she turned her face away, laughing.

"And when you die of exhaustion, we could hide your body and divvy up the oil leases," she finished for him.

"Oh, *Abby.*" He buried his laughing face in her neck and his fervent hug robbed her of breath for a moment. "Let me touch you . . . just a little. I'm starving for you."

His voice sounded so wistful, she had already begun to lean into him when sanity returned and she gasped at her weakness. "Joe Gilbraithe! You can't mean that you're thinking about petting in the school broom closet?"

He inhaled roughly. "If you knew what I was really thinking, you would probably slap my face," he said throatily.

Her hands moved across his back, testing the hard flesh. When she spoke, the words came out in a breathless whisper. "What are you thinking?"

"I'm an animal," he said woefully as he nibbled on her earlobe. "I'm nothing but a disgusting animal."

"*Tell* me," she demanded with a small laugh. "I happen to be particularly fond of animals."

"If I could do what I want to do, I would push you against the wall." He was feasting on her neck as he spoke, his movements becoming urgent. "Then I would raise your skirt . . ." He paused to press one full breast upward so he could kiss the rounded top that appeared in the V of her blouse. His other hand searched under her skirt and slid inside the top of her panties, his long fingers spreading across the gently rounded flesh of her stomach.

"And?" she prompted with an impatient whisper.

"Abby!" He lifted his head and she could feel him trying to see her face in the dark. "You don't really want me to go on, do you?"

"I was just curious," she muttered, feeling the heat in her face grow. When she heard his delighted laughter, she grabbed his neck and gave him a shake. "You have a terrible effect on me," she accused lovingly. "We always make love in the strangest places."

"We don't seem to be making love at all," he said regretfully. "This is the first time we've been alone in weeks and we're *talking*."

Joe was a man of action, and before she could reply, he took action to remedy their sad situation. Except for a breathless sigh, there was only silence in the broom closet for the next few minutes.

But all too soon the morning bell rang, bringing a harsh groan from deep inside his throat. He sighed roughly and smoothed down her hair with fingers that shook only slightly. "Time to go, my sweet."

She leaned against him for a moment in disappointment, unwilling to let him go so soon. Then, as her pulse slowed, she moved away and began to refasten her blouse. After they had hastily straightened their clothing, Joe peeked around the door, then signaled for her to come out.

As she stepped into the hallway, Abby heard a delighted "Gotcha!" behind her and turned to see identical leers on the faces of Larry and Roy.

"So we've been necking in the broom closet, have we?" Larry asked, his face held in stern lines. "What do you think of that kind of conduct, Roy?"

Roy studied Joe's grinning face. "I think I'm going to bring my wife up here and show her the broom closet."

"That's just the kind of kinky thing you would do," Abby said, giving him a squelching glare.

Roy raised one brow inquisitively. "Have you been getting kinky in the closet, Joe?"

"I tried, Roy," Joe said, shaking his head in sorrow. "I really tried."

Before Joe could give them any more encouragement, a young woman called to Larry and both men moved away, still grinning widely.

"Why can't I have nice ordinary friends like other people?" she moaned. "If those two weren't both happily married, they would be standing on a street corner somewhere, calling 'Hey, chickie, chickie' to every woman that walked by."

Joe laughed. "I like them. They're funny."

"And so amazingly lifelike," she muttered. Then, catching his eye, she began to laugh. "Okay, I'll admit it. I like them too. I just can't figure out why." She looked up at him and sighed. "I guess we had better get to class before the kids decide to take over the school."

"Tonight," he said softly, the single word a promise. "Tonight, after the kids are asleep, at least I'll be able to kiss you again."

He touched her hand with one finger, a soft caress that no one could possibly have noticed, but that meant so much to her. Then he was striding down the hall away from her.

*   *   *

"No, Jones!" Joe shouted at the tall, heavily built boy. "Not right. Left. Do you know left, Jones? Show me your left hand." He nodded when the grinning boy promptly lifted his hand. "Very good. Now let's do it again and this time let's see you cut *left*."

Joe ran down the side of the practice field, keeping up with the play, watching every move. At the other end of the field, a blond boy, more slender than the others, practiced running maneuvers. His name was Tim Perkins and he was Joe's secret weapon.

Perkins had played in only two of the game films that Joe had viewed, but two had been enough to tell him what he needed to know. The boy had something. And if handled right, he had the speed and style necessary to make all the difference in future games.

In years past, Coach Hemp, Bardle's retired football coach, had concentrated almost entirely on a passing game. Joe was slowly, carefully changing the emphasis to a running game. Not only would the move take all of the Bulldogs' old opponents by surprise, but it also gave the boys a feeling that they had gained a secret weapon. And that was the impetus they needed to have a winning team.

As he watched over his team, Joe felt satisfaction and even excitement growing inside him. It was like watching a flower bloom.

Suddenly his eyes noticed a small figure on one of the benches, braids hanging—evenly this time—over her shoulders. Waving to Brennie, he signaled to the team to head for the showers; then, wiping his face with the towel that hung around his neck, he walked toward her.

"Hi, sweetheart," he said, sitting down beside her. "What do you think of the team?"

"I think the one in the gray sweatshirt is cute," she said without hesitation.

He chuckled. "You think that will give us a better chance of winning?"

She grinned up at him. "It couldn't hurt."

"Did you stop by to walk me home?" He was escorted to Abby's house each day by either Brennie or Jeff.

She shrugged. "I just wanted to watch and Mom said I could stay until you finished."

He stared down at her for a minute. "Honey, is something wrong? You look a little pale. Maybe you shouldn't be out here in this sun."

"It's not that hot." Her lower lip drooped in a pout that was completely out of character.

Brennie had never been as uncomplicated as Jeff, but neither was she a sulky child. "Have you been home since school let out?" he asked.

She shook her head, avoiding his eyes.

"So your mother hasn't seen you since this morning?"

She started to shake her head again, then leaned it against him instead. "Joe, I really don't feel too good. I've got a terrible stomachache." She didn't take her head away from his shoulder, but turned it to look up at him. "It was the party yesterday, I think."

"Pigged out, did you?"

She nodded. "Six brownies and a whole pizza," she said sorrowfully. "I didn't feel too hot this morning, but I didn't want to tell Mom because she would've made me take something totally disgusting."

He stood, pulling her up with him. "I think the time has come for the disgusting stuff, don't you?"

They walked off the practice field together, but before they had gotten more than a block away, Brennie suddenly doubled over, moaning in her high child's voice.

Scooping her up in his arms, Joe carried her quickly toward Abby's house. When he leaned his head down to reassure her, he felt the heat in her face and all his muscles tightened in fear.

Although the house was only two blocks away from the high school, it seemed to Joe to take forever to walk that last block.

Abby must have seen them from the window, for she met them on the porch. "What happened?" she asked, anxiously reaching for her daughter. "Is she hurt?"

"She says it's just a stomachache, but she's running a fever." He kept his voice carefully calm, unwilling to let her see his uncertainty.

Abby walked ahead of him, holding the door open. "Let's get her to bed, then I'll call Dr. Harding."

In Brennie's bedroom, Joe laid her down on the bed and stared down at her in concern. "Brennie, honey, do you mind if I poke you a little?"

"Joe—" Abby began, fear showing in her eyes and her voice.

"Just a second, Abby." When Brennie shook her head, he pressed softly on her abdomen, then lower and lower until he reached the spot that brought a gasp of pain from the girl.

He glanced up at Abby and nodded, confirming her fears. "I think we should go ahead and take her in, Abby. Why don't you call Harding and tell him we're coming?"

Five minutes later they were in the station wagon on their way to the hospital. Jeff shared the front seat with Joe while Abby held Brennie's head in her lap in the back. No one spoke. Even Jeff seemed unusually subdued.

Doctor Harding was at the hospital when they arrived and immediately took Brennie away to examine her. Joe stood impatiently at the window of the waiting room for a moment, staring at the parking lot with unseeing eyes.

Suddenly, with a word to Jeff and Abby, he left them sitting on the green plastic sofa and began to hunt for the coffee machine. He simply couldn't sit quietly and wait.

All his life when something needed to be done Joe had gone and done it. That's all there was to it, he thought. He had merely determined what action was necessary and then he'd taken it. Never had he felt the kind of helplessness he felt now. There was absolutely nothing he could do except wait, and it was driving him crazy.

Suddenly Joe realized what he was doing. He was so busy concentrating on his own fears that he was forgetting there was something he could do, something he had to do. Maybe not for Brennie; he had to leave her in the doctor's hands, but he could be there for Abby and Jeff.

He carried two cups of coffee back to the waiting room. Setting them on the coffee table, he lowered himself onto the couch and picked up both of Abby's hands, squeezing them tightly between his.

"Joe, she looked so fragile when they took her away." Abby's voice was only a thin, high whisper.

"She's a normal, healthy girl, Abby," he said, willing certainty into his voice. "Nowadays appendectomies are considered routine. She'll be fine."

At that moment Dr. Harding stepped into the waiting room and they rose expectantly. "You were right, Joe," he said calmly. "It's the appendix. And I'm afraid we'll have to take it out now. It's already ruptured."

He gave Abby a reassuring glance. "We could wait for the tests to confirm that, but I don't see any need. Of course, it's up to you."

"No—no," Abby said, her voice distracted. "You do whatever you think is right."

He nodded, then smiled. "Would you like to see her before we prep her?"

"Could we?" Abby asked urgently.

Joe's heart ached for her. She sounded so feverishly grateful for the doctor's consideration. His arm tightened around her waist as they walked down the hall together.

In the sterile hospital bed, Brennie looked even more fragile. She glanced at them as they walked into the room and tears formed in her eyes, eyes so much like Abby's, Joe thought.

"Brennie," Abby said, smiling as she moved toward the bed. "Brennie, honey, you're going to be just fine. Dr. Harding says so."

"I'm scared, Mama."

Joe had never heard Brennie call her mother Mama. It did something to him. Standing at her other side, he picked up her hand. "Brennie, can I tell you a secret?" She nodded slowly. "I'm a lot older than you are. I've had a dozen operations and every single time I was scared."

"Honest?"

"Honest," he said, nodding. "There's nothing wrong with being afraid. Just remember that your mother and I wouldn't let anyone do anything to you that was wrong."

She gave him a small, hesitant smile. Then the nurse appeared in the doorway and they knew it was time to leave.

As they walked back to the waiting room, he said, "Abby, I hate the thought of leaving you, but don't you think Jeff would be better off spending the night with Harrison and Judy?"

"Yes," she said wearily. "Yes, of course you're right. I didn't think of that."

She looked up and seemed to recognize the concern in his eyes. "Don't worry," she said, smiling. "I'll be fine. And so will Brennie. You go ahead and take care of Jeff."

He knew she was right, but he couldn't help glancing over his shoulder at her as he and Jeff left the hospital.

His mind was so taken up with Abby and Brennie that for a long while Joe didn't notice the unusual silence in the car. When he did, he said softly, "She really will be all right, Jeff."

After a moment Jeff answered in a small voice, "A couple of weeks ago I teased her about getting breasts and last night I put a frog in her bed."

Joe chuckled, reaching over to give him a reassuring hug. "That's all a part of being a brother. I'll bet Brennie understands that."

"She didn't act like she understood last night,"

Jeff said ruefully, then grinned. "Brennie yells louder than anyone I know."

They laughed together and Joe could feel the boy relax. Suddenly he looked up and studied Joe's face intently.

"Something else bothering you?"

He didn't take his eyes off Joe as he said bluntly, "People are saying that you're going to marry Mom."

Joe sighed roughly. He and Abby should have known that the rumors would eventually get back to the children. Without taking his eyes off the road, Joe said, "Would you mind . . . if it were the truth?"

"No," he said slowly. "I don't think so. When I first heard about it, I thought it would be super having a football player for a father, but then I thought . . . well, you're a football player to everybody. See?"

"I think so. You mean a father should be different to a son than he is to everyone else."

"Yeah." Jeff stared at him as though expecting an instant answer.

Drawing a bracing breath, Joe gave it a try. "When your mother and I get married, then it will be different. Aren't we friends now?"

He nodded.

"Well, just think how much more special it will be when we all live together. You'll stop thinking of me as a football player and I won't be the father of any of the other guys."

"Yeah," Jeff said, his eyes growing bright. "None of the other guys will be there when you belch after dinner or anything."

Joe's shoulders shook with laughter. "I don't

think your mother will allow too much belching, but you've got the right idea."

"Joe," Jeff said after a thoughtful moment. "Will I call you Dad?"

This was the question Joe had been dreading for weeks. "Do you want to?" he asked finally.

"I don't know," Jeff said slowly, then added, "But if I do, it won't mean that I've forgotten about Daddy."

Joe couldn't speak for a second. Then, when they pulled into Judy and Harrison's driveway, he turned and looked down at Jeff. "I know that, son. I don't want you to forget him."

Jeff stared up at him, eyes wide, then suddenly threw his thin arms around Joe's waist. Before Joe could react, he was out of the car, running to meet Harry, who stood in the doorway.

Joe felt a strange glow as he drove back to the hospital. Jeff was glad. He was really pleased that Abby and he were going to be married. It was as if a tremendous weight had been lifted from Joe's shoulders.

The feeling sustained him through the waiting period of Brennie's operation. When Dr. Harding walked into the room to tell them that Brennie had come through it just fine, he felt that nothing could ever go wrong again.

They waited for a while to see Brennie when she came out from under the anesthetic. Then Joe insisted that Abby go home to sleep. Although she looked relieved and very happy, he could tell she was exhausted.

As they walked in the front door, she suddenly turned to him and laughed.

"What's funny?" he said, pulling her into his arms as soon as the door closed behind them.

"I was just thinking about what Jeff told me in the waiting room."

He smoothed the hair back from her forehead with two fingers. "What did he say?"

She glanced up at him ruefully. "You'll remember that I was a little upset?" He nodded. "I kept saying I couldn't understand how something like this could happen to someone as healthy as Brennie, and Jeff looked up at me with those big, solemn eyes and said, 'When you grow up you know that some questions don't have answers.'" Abby laughed again. "I couldn't believe it. I just sat there looking at him with my mouth hanging open like an idiot." She shook her head. "Jeff has never been one to philosophize."

Joe smiled a slow, secret smile. "Maybe he's just growing up."

"Maybe," she said quietly, then she shuddered. "Joe, I never really thought about how very much of my life was taken up with the kids. Not until you came along. Now I wonder why I didn't see it before. Someday they'll leave. That's part of life. And the emptiness that I would have faced then is terrible to think about."

She grinned suddenly. "Of course, I have no intention of saving you for my old age. You're pretty handy to have around right now. And I'm not the only one who thinks so. If you listen to Brennie and Jeff, you single-handedly built the seven wonders of the world."

He smiled slightly. "They do seem to be accepting me, don't they?"

"Accepting you?" she asked incredulously. "Joe, they love you."

He ran his fingers through his hair. "I've been afraid for a long time now, Abby. Afraid I wouldn't measure up to what a father should be." He laughed shortly. "I was so sure I would screw up with them."

"But you're wonderful with them. I think you have some crazy ideas about being a father," she said. "No one expects perfection. Show me someone who says he's the perfect father and I'll show you a liar. You love them, and that's what's important."

She sat down on the couch and pulled him down beside her. "I guess we don't always show you how much we need you. I think tonight has made me realize just how much." She touched his face and smiled. "Even if I didn't love you to distraction, I'd still keep you."

Joe became statue-still at her words, then slowly closed his eyes and let the waves of intense emotion wash over him. After a moment he opened them and whispered hoarsely, "I thought you would never say it." Burying his face in her neck, he inhaled the precious scent of her. "Sweet heaven, I thought you would never say it."

Abby couldn't believe what she was hearing. Framing his face with her hands, she pulled his head up, her eyes startled as she stared at him. "Joe," she said in a harsh whisper, "you mean you didn't *know*?"

When he shook his head, she felt tears of pain form in her eyes. "I've done it again," she said, her voice heavy with self-accusation. "Dammit, I've done it again. I love you more than anything on earth and all I ever seem to do is hurt you."

"No," he said, shushing her with a finger on her lips. "Don't say that. Don't even think it. You've given me more than I could ever have imagined."

He pulled her head down to his shoulder and continued in a whisper. "There have been times in the last few weeks, sweetheart, that I felt if I couldn't have you and the kids, I wouldn't survive. But I would have. People have a way of surviving." He gently turned her face to him. "I would have survived, Abby, but I would have been empty. All the good parts, the worthwhile parts of me belong to you."

Without any conscious movement they had begun to slide lower on the couch until they lay together, side by side, their bodies straining to become one.

Suddenly he smiled at her and the sun shone out of his dark eyes. "So if you don't want to be haunted by an empty shell, you'd better keep me."

She couldn't speak; her heart was too full. Her only response was to pull his head down to hers, and the dreadful waiting was ended at last.

Joe glanced up at the scoreboard and continued pacing back and forth on the sidelines. It was the last down of the fourth quarter and the score was tied. This was the moment the whole town had been waiting months for.

It hadn't been an easy season. They had slid through it by the skin of their teeth, taking some devastating losses, but also coming up with some brilliant wins.

The instability of the team was what worried Joe most. The other team on the field had the same win-loss record as Bardle. The team that won tonight would go on to the state play-offs. And he was very much afraid that the winning team wouldn't be the Bardle Bulldogs.

He watched the seconds ticking away and knew that he had done everything he could possibly do. The Bulldogs had no time-outs remaining. They would have to pass, he thought. That worried him. Perkins was a running magician, but he was not always in the right place at the right time.

Joe held his breath when he saw the quarterback drop back for a pass with only four seconds left on the clock. "Perkins," he said under his breath as he caught sight of the wide receiver, "Perkins, dammit, you're not deep enough. Keep going!" Then louder, "Keep going!"

It was beautiful. It was as if he were behind the boy guiding him. Perkins slipped into position as smooth as silk and suddenly the ball was in his arms and he was running, showing everyone the rhythmic stride that had already brought college scouts to Bardle.

Joe could feel the tension mounting, hear the intensity of the screams from the crowd as Perkins sidestepped man after man on the field.

Then, with a seemingly effortless movement, he was over the goal line and the town of Bardle, Texas, went wild. Joe threw his hat in the air and turned to watch the stands.

Harrison and Judy were there, their arms clasped around each other as they jumped up and down clumsily in their excitement. He saw Larry and Roy ecstatically showering the crowd with popcorn. Even Eb was there, his gnarled wooden cane waving frantically in the air as he tried to ignore the small, scolding woman at his side.

Joe felt excitement and pride shoot through him in a wild burst of adrenaline. Then, as his gaze dropped, he saw three figures running down the crowded field toward him.

The crowd receded into the background and he moved forward to meet the three most important people in the world. Joe knew that he had found it at last. The winning team was finally his.

EDITOR'S CORNER

LOVE LIFTS US UP WHERE WE BELONG!

You'll be seeing these words a lot in the next six months in advertisements in major women's magazines and other publications. We've adopted this slogan for our second anniversary which we celebrate with the publication of next month's LOVESWEPTS. And we think it's just right! LOVE LIFTS US UP WHERE WE BELONG expresses the reactions of readers to LOVESWEPT romances while describing the performance of our books on chain and independent bookstore bestseller lists.

Now, as we enter our third year of publication, I want to thank everyone who has helped create this remarkable line: you who buy the books, our wonderful authors, and, of course, my colleagues at Bantam, all of whom are first-rate. Especially, though, I must single out the contributions of the LOVESWEPT staff—Susann Koenig, Elizabeth Barrett and Barbara Alpert. Their enthusiasm, excitement, and energy are as high today as when we worked on the first manuscript we purchased for LOVESWEPT. Happy birthday to us all!

Now to the treats in store for you next month.

Sara Orwig is back with a simply wonderful love story, **CALHOUN AND KID**, LOVESWEPT #91. An ornery hero (who is also a hunk, by the way), Jared Calhoun plagues Courtney Meade. Single parents with sons the same age, Jared and Courtney would seem to have everything in common, yet their personalities appear to be completely at odds. She's shy and sweet; he's forward and crusty. It's double trouble from the moment they meet and Courtney gets the blame for Jared being shot in the foot! Then it's more merry and sensuous excitement as they reconcile their feuding boys and set about reforming one another . . . in the most delightful ways! This is another heartwarming story from our own Sara Orwig who just keeps topping herself with every book she writes!

We are delighted to welcome Carole Nelson Douglas as a LOVESWEPT author. A marvelously versatile writer, Carole is known for her historical and science fiction novels. How glad we are to have tempted her to do her first short contemporary romance for us because **AZURE DAYS, QUICKSILVER NIGHTS**, LOVESWEPT #92, is a fabulous love story. Set in Monte Carlo and on the Riviera amidst the rich, the famous, the dangerous, **AZURE DAYS, QUICKSILVER NIGHTS** is the dramatic story of Chrystal Remy, heiress to a crumbling villa and a mountain of debts, and the magnetic Damon Vance, a man known in international art circles for his expertise . . . and mystery. Both have known tragic first marriages, both know what they could mean to one another, but intriguing secrets keep them apart—while forcing them together. **AZURE DAYS, QUICKSILVER NIGHTS** is a memorable contribution to the LOVESWEPT series and a love story you won't soon forget. (Incidentally, some of the exquisite antique clothes described in the book come from Carole's own wardrobe . . . and how I covet those gorgeous creations!)

I guarantee you'll be absolutely charmed by **PRACTICE MAKES PERFECT**, LOVESWEPT #93, by Kathleen Downes. This is Kathleen's second LOVESWEPT and it is a double delight. Pippi and Jeremy are best friends. Unlucky in love, Pippi has always relied on Jeremy . . . and his strong shoulder to cry on. Out of the blue he asks her to help him figure out how to court the woman he loves . . . and Pippi's emotional world turns upside down. She never knew she could be so distressed . . . or enthralled. As their "rehearsals" become more intimate, Pippi finds herself in a dilemma. You'll relish the deviousness of a darling man and the woman he would make his darling, so be sure to read **PRACTICES MAKES PERFECT**! It's fun, it's frolicksome, it's wonderfully touching.

There's humor galore plus sensuous magic in **WAITING FOR PRINCE CHARMING**, LOVESWEPT #94, by Joan Elliott Pickart. You'll revel in the romance of Chelsey Star and Mitch Brannon, two of the most lovable characters in Joan's extensive repertoire. Chelsey is hardly the traditional Cinderella waiting for a fairy godmother; she's an active, vital modern woman. But it *is* glass that brings her together with her Prince Charming—not the glass of a slipper, but of a broken windshield on Mitch's fabulously expensive, brand-new sports car. And there aren't any evil stepsisters here—just a group of wonderful humans and animals who delightfully propel and complicate Mitch and Chelsey's loving fairytale. Another real winner from Joan Elliott Pickart!

Again, thank you for your wonderful support for the last two years. You can count on us to do our very best always to give you the very best in romance novels!

Sincerely,

Carolyn Nichols

Carolyn Nichols
  Editor
LOVESWEPT
Bantam Books, Inc.
666 Fifth Avenue
New York, NY 10103

Read this special preview of

THE FOREVER DREAM

---

by Iris Johansen

Coming in May 1985 from Bantam Books

HE PROMISES NOTHING LESS THAN LOVE
WITHOUT END . . .

Exquisite, radiant Tania Orlinov—incomparable prima ballerina, renowned Soviet defector—she expresses the dreams of love only dance can reveal . . . but seeks none of them for herself.

Brilliant, mysterious Jared Ryker—an uncommon man with extraordinary vision, a gifted genetic scientist—he holds the key to an astonishing secret . . . and yearns to share it with one special woman.

She has become his obsession. He longs to possess her with an enduring passion that time can never destroy. But when she is brought to him against her will by those who covet his secret, Jared is torn by need . . . and seduced by her beauty. Inevitably, desire flames between them—stunning them both with its depth and intensity. But their private fantasy is shattered—by men determined to seize Jared's research and control its power. Until, in a fierce confrontation set against a windswept mountain's splendor, Jared and Tania must fight for their lives . . . and for their freedom to build a future in each other's arms. . . .

Iris Johansen's
THE FOREVER DREAM

*D*amn this moonlight! Was it only last night she had blamed the full moon for her temporary madness? She was going to blame it for considerably more than that if those clouds didn't oblige. She needed the cover of darkness to cross the courtyard and get around the curve in the road before the guard completed his rounds.

She shrank against the stone wall, deep in shadow. Her gaze was fixed worriedly on the sky, watching the clouds; they approached the moon with a laziness that stretched her nerves to the limit. The guard should be back around to the courtyard in another four minutes, according to her calculations. She'd spent three hours here in the shadows four nights ago, observing and timing the guard's movements. If she hadn't had an opportunity to sneak into the back of the van, she'd wanted to be prepared to go out on foot, as she was doing now . . . as she *would* be doing now if those clouds would just cover the moon. She bit her lip in frustration. She didn't dare leave the shadows until the moon was obscured, and she must at least be across the courtyard before the guard rounded the north wall. She couldn't chance his being in the courtyard for the short time it would take her to get around the curve of the road.

Only three minutes to go. With one hand she tugged at the collar of her turtleneck sweater beneath the dark jacket while she clutched a coil of rope in the other. Move, damn you, she commanded the clouds. With maddening slowness, they drifted across the bright sphere, bringing the welcome darkness.

She flew out of the shadows like an arrow shot from a battlement in the chateau long ago, the rubber soles of her tennis shoes skimming over the rough cobbles with sure swiftness. By the time she reached the road she had only one minute to go before the guard would reappear, and already those blasted clouds were rolling through the skies as if fleeing the moon.

She streaked down the road, her braid flying out in back of her and her breath laboring in her lungs as she raced the cloud that could mean her escape or capture. She lost. She was a full fifty yards from the curve in the road when the moonlight suddenly flooded the road with the clarity of daylight. She felt the remaining breath leave her body, and she hesitated for a moment, as if that moonlight were an actual blow striking her. Lord, it was as bright as a spotlight, and the guard should be rounding the wall right now.

She hadn't thought she could go any faster, but the sudden burst of adrenaline that panic released proved her wrong. Let him be late, she prayed frantically, or let him be thinking of something else. Let him stop for a cigarette, or be looking anywhere but at the road. At any moment she expected to hear a shout and the sound of feet pounding heavily on the cobblestones behind her, but there was no sound except the sharp gasps of her own breathing. Then she'd rounded the curve in the road and was out of sight of the chateau!

Relief washed over her with a force that made her head swim. The first difficulty was overcome and she was on her way. She slowed her steps and then came to a complete halt. Her heart was pounding painfully in her breast and her knees felt weak as butter from reaction. Now that the first bit was out of the way she had to regain control of her nerves, twitching from the tension produced by the precarious cloud cover. There was still the checkpoint to get past and the rest of the road to the valley to cross before she was free.

Her pace slowed to a walk, and she hugged the inner side of the road, taking as much shelter as she could from the foliage on the side of the cliff. Heaven knew there was little enough to hug, she thought dispiritedly. The road seemed to be cut out of the mountain itself here—a bluff on one side, a sloping verge of perhaps five or six yards on the other side. From the edge of the verge it was a sheer drop to the valley below. But the verge was the key to her escape. She'd noticed there was a sparse straggle of trees on it near the checkpoint. With any luck she'd be able to use them as cover to slip past the chain link barricade across the road. Despite the moonlight, they should provide enough shadow for her to avoid being seen if she were careful. But that steeply sloping terrain was going to prove tricky. On her previous reconnaissance she'd detected little or no ground cover on the verge, and keeping her footing on an incline that steep until she reached the stand of pines was going to be nearly impossible. Her lips curved in a wry smile as she recalled her words to Jared only two weeks ago. Surefooted or not, she might well fall off this bloody mountain.

Well, that was why she'd brought the rope and the grappling hook, wasn't it? She could secure the rope around her waist and use the grappling hook on the trees, working her way from one to another across that sloping verge until she was past the checkpoint and it was safe to crawl back up on the road.

She'd been expecting it, but her heart still lurched when she came around the bend and saw the brilliant glow of the Coleman lanterns about fifty yards ahead. She instinctively shrank closer to the bluff while her gaze swiftly searched the scene ahead for an alternate route that wouldn't be as risky.

Two steel posts anchored the chain barrier stretched across the road. And the two guards who patrolled it were lounging on the bluff side of the road playing cards, leaning against the padded seats of their overturned motorcycles. She could hear their voices in the clear mountain air, and it gave her a little shock. They sounded so close she might have been right next to them. At least their lanterns were on the bluff side of the road, and if their game was interesting enough, it might take their attention off any noise she might make as she crawled past them. It was difficult to tell from this distance, but she didn't think they were the same guards who had brought her back to the chateau yesterday. In fact, neither one was familiar to her, and she'd thought she'd run across every security guard on the place at one time or another in the past two weeks.

Well, she couldn't stay here all night gawking at them. It was obvious the physical setup hadn't altered, and she was just going to have to keep to her original plan. She took the rope and grappling hook from her shoulder and checked the knot she'd tied in the steel loop of the hook to make sure it was tight, then dropped the grappling hook on the ground while she knotted the other end about her waist with equal care.

There was a burst of laughter from the men playing cards, and it caused her to jump with surprise. She drew a deep breath and forced herself to relax. Easy. This was just a piece of cake, remember? She was going to have to be very cool and certain in the next few minutes, and unsteady nerves would not help her.

She picked up the grappling hook and waited patiently until the clouds once more obscured the moon before dashing across the road and crouching on the edge of the verge for a moment. Then she slowly slid down onto the verge itself, carefully holding on to the trunk of the tree closest to the road. Oh, Lord, it was going to be worse than she'd thought. The earth slid out from under her, and she had to clutch desperately at the pine to keep from sliding with it. The ground seemed to be composed of nothing but loose dirt and shale—it was a wonder it even supported the scraggly pines that bordered the road. Still holding the trunk of the tree with one arm, she cautiously brought the grappling hook into play, reaching as far as she could and fastening it to the tree nearest her. Thank heaven the distance between most of the trees wasn't over two or three feet. It was a relatively simple matter to slip the hook around each slender trunk and then pull herself painstakingly hand over hand to the tree itself.

Once she became accustomed to the tempo of the procedure, her progress was much more rapid, and if she hadn't needed to be stealthy, she'd have been able to cover the fifty yards or so in a relatively short time. As it was, it took her almost twenty minutes to draw even with the barricade. She paused for a minute to catch her breath and wipe her chafed hands on her jeans before taking a fresh grip on the rope. With only the width of the road separating her from the two guards, she could feel her breath constrict in her lungs and the muscles of her stomach knot with tension. She could practically hear them breathe, she thought nervously. One false move and they'd be sure to hear her and react with the efficient swiftness Betz's security men always displayed.

But there wasn't going to be a false move. All she needed to do was to continue as she'd started, and in a few minutes she'd be safe. With the utmost caution she negotiated the next two trees, and she was past the checkpoint! Only a few yards past it, but it was a victory nonetheless.

Her swift surge of triumph was abruptly stemmed as she disengaged the hook and prepared to move on. The closest pine was over four yards away! The shock and dismay she felt almost caused her to let go of the tree she was clinging to. There was no possibility she'd be able to lean that far to slip the hook around the trunk. Damn it, just when she was almost home free. She bit her lips, anxiously trying to think of a way out. There was only one, and it was so risky that she hesitated to attempt it. She'd have to toss the hook and hope to encircle the base of the pine. In the darkness her chances of succeeding weren't all that great, and even if she did, the noise might give her away. Well, she really had no choice.

She just wished that she'd paid more attention when Tyler had wanted to teach her the fine art of pitching horseshoes, that weekend at the farm.

Her eyes straining in the darkness to gauge the distance, she balanced the hook in her hand as if it were a boomerang. Then, with a murmured prayer on her lips, she let the hook fly through the air. Had she made it?

But suddenly it no longer mattered. If the loud clang as the hook hit the shale hadn't given her away, the minor rockslide that resulted certainly had.

"What the hell was that?" One of the guards jumped to his feet, grabbing for a lantern.

There was nothing left to do but run for it. Her hands ripping frantically at the knot at her waist, she scrambled to her feet and lurched forward, trying desperately to regain the road.

Strangely, she didn't hear the crash of the shot until after she felt the first burning pain rip through her. She knew an instant of wild regret, more poignant than anything she'd ever experienced. Then there was only stark terror as she pitched forward, rolling like a broken toy down the sloping incline and off the edge of the cliff into the darkness beyond.

"Dr. Ryker, are you awake? It's essential that I speak to you." The knocking on his door was repeated with a persistence that belied the politeness of Betz's words.

How the hell could he help but be awake? Jared sat up in bed and leaned over to the bedside table to switch on the lamp. He'd just begun to drop off when Betz had started that damned knocking, and being wakened didn't improve a disposition that was on the raw anyway. "Come in, Betz. It had better be 'essential.'"

"I think you know by now I'd never disturb you for anything that wasn't extremely important." There was a touch of indignation in his ponderous voice.

"Get on with it, Betz," Jared said wearily. "You're here now. Let's have it."

"I'm afraid you may be quite upset, Dr. Ryker. There's been a slight difficulty regarding Miss Orlinov."

The impatience and annoyance vanished as the anxiety that was always latent in him these days surfaced rapidly. "Slight difficulty?" His voice was carefully neutral, his gaze sharp as a laser. "And just what do you consider slight, Betz?"

"She's been shot." Then, as Jared inhaled sharply and his face turned white, he continued hurriedly. "It's only a flesh wound in the shoulder. Liston assures me there was no serious damage done."

Jared threw back the covers and leaped out of bed, his every move charged with electricity. "Where is she?"

"He didn't intend to hit her—it was only meant to be a warning shot. He was startled when she appeared so suddenly at the checkpoint."

"The checkpoint? Is that where she is?" Why the hell hadn't he realized she'd try something like this? She'd been almost feverishly gay at dinner, and that should have signaled him that she was hiding something. Now she'd been hurt, and who knew how badly? My God, what if the bullet had severed an artery? She could bleed to death before he could even get there.

Betz was nodding. "Liston radioed word to me from the checkpoint by mobile phone and I dispatched the van to bring her back to the chateau." He paused. "I told them to wait to transport her until you arrived on the scene."

Jared grabbed a shirt and pants from the armoire. "I'll need the medical bag you'll find in the closet in the bathroom," he said crisply. "You have the jeep waiting?"

Betz moved obediently toward the door of the master bath. "Yes, of course. This is all very regrettable, Dr. Ryker. It *was* an accident, you realize."

"It may be more regrettable than you know." Jared's voice was icy, but there was sheer savagery in his granite-hard face. "Because if she's really badly hurt, I'm going to throw your man Liston off this son of a bitch of a mountain. I just may do it anyway. And then I'll start on you, Betz." He turned and left the bedroom, striding through the corridors and down the stairs.

The jeep was in the courtyard as Betz had promised. Jared looked grim as he swung up into the passenger seat. He drew a deep, calming breath. He mustn't give in to this rage that was tearing through him. He'd need all the cool steadiness he could muster when he saw how badly she was hurt.

Betz came hurrying out the courtyard door, carefully placed the brown cowhide medical bag he was carrying in the back, and slid into the driver's seat. "Sorry to have kept you waiting. I took the precaution of asking Dr. Jeffers to fly in immediately in case he was needed."

Jared tensed. "You told me it was only a flesh wound."

"I'm sure it is," Betz said quickly as he started the engine and put the jeep in gear. "It's just a precaution, Dr. Ryker."

"It'd better be, Betz," Jared said softly, his tone as menacing as a cocked pistol. "If I were you, I'd be praying very hard that it is."

The security man shrugged. He reversed the jeep with precision and drove out the arched gate of the courtyard. "In a few minutes you'll be able to judge for yourself."

The checkpoint was teeming with activity and lights when they rounded the curve. Betz halted the jeep directly before the van and was immediately approached by a tall young man in a leather jacket who burst hurriedly into speech. "It wasn't our fault, Mr. Betz. She hopped up out of the trees and surprised us. We didn't even know who she was. All we saw was a shadow."

"And do you always shoot at shadows?" Jared bit out.

The man moistened his lips nervously as his gaze took in Jared's taut face and blazing eyes. "Not always, sir. But in this case we were told to shoot first and ask questions later, because your safety was paramount. We were only following orders, Dr. Ryker."

"Where is she?" He had to make sure that Tania was all right before he gave himself the pleasure of taking the man apart limb from limb.

The man answered quickly. "We've put her in the back of the van. I've rigged up a bandage for her shoulder, and the bleeding has stopped. She's unconscious now, but she fainted only when I was applying the bandage." He turned. "I'll take you to her."

"Let's go," Jared said crisply. He got out of the jeep and strode rapidly toward the back of the van.

When Jared reached the back of the van, one glance told him that Betz's very valuable man was extremely close to being permanently mutilated. "My God, her clothes are torn to shreds. What the hell have you done to her? You lying bastard, if I find out you've raped her, I'll chop you into little pieces." He dropped to his knees beside Tania. "Where did she get all these bruises?"

"We didn't touch her," Liston protested desperately. He swallowed hard and then proceeded more calmly. "Those are rope burns. When she was shot, she rolled down the incline and over the edge of the cliff. She'd been using a grappling hook on the trees, to inch her way past the checkpoint, and the rope was still knotted about her waist when she rolled over the edge of the cliff. The rope kept her from falling to the valley below, but naturally the jerk bruised her quite a bit." He tried to smile. "Donalson and I tried to be as careful as we could when we pulled her back to the verge, but there wasn't any way we could prevent her from getting a little scraped. She was lucky as hell to come out of it as well as she did."

Lucky. Jared felt the muscles of his stomach tighten at the vivid picture Liston's terse words evoked. Tania dangling hundreds of feet in the air from a slender rope and two trigger-happy idiots the only hope she had of survival. It made him sick even to think about it. Lord, yes, she'd been lucky.

"You say she was still conscious when you were bandaging her wound?" Jared asked thickly. He hoped not. It must have been sheer hell for her if she'd been totally aware during that nightmarish experience.

Liston nodded eagerly. "She was conscious the entire time until we were trying to get her jacket off. She was even able to help a little while we were hauling her up the cliff." He knelt beside Ryker and pushed aside the torn sweater to reveal a crude bandage fashioned of brown plaid flannel, obviously torn from a shirt. "See, the bleeding's stopped entirely. The bullet just grazed her shoulder, clean as a whistle."

"Get your hands off her!" Liston jumped as if he'd been flicked with a whip and backed hurriedly away. Jared drew a deep breath and tried to submerge the anger that had suddenly exploded. "Just get out of here, Liston. Now!"

The guard didn't have to be told twice. As the man jumped out of the van Ryker didn't give him a second glance. His gaze was fixed intently on Tania's shoulder.

"Clean as a whistle," he repeated disgustedly. "She'll be lucky if she doesn't get blood poisoning," Jared said grimly, carefully cutting away the flannel bandage. His hands were remarkably steady, he noticed absently. It was a wonder, when he was shaking so inside. He hadn't felt as helpless as this since the night Lita died. But he wasn't helpless now. He had knowledge and experience on his side. He had to remember that. He hadn't been able to help Lita then, but he could help Tania now.

He soon discovered Liston was right. Though the wound looked ugly and inflamed, the bullet had just grazed the fleshy part of the shoulder. He breathed a sigh of relief as he quickly removed the bandage and reached for an antiseptic. He carefully cleaned the wound before rebandaging it with sterile gauze and taping it firmly.

"That's all I can do for her now. I'll give her a shot to ease the pain, and antibiotic and tetanus injections. After that it's up to your doctor to do his stuff. Now let's get her back to the chateau. Tell the driver I want the ride to be pure velvet. If he jars her even a little, I'll break his neck. Understand?"

"You needn't worry. I've already warned him to be most careful." Betz disappeared from view, and a moment later Jared could hear his voice at the front of the van.

Taking off his jacket, Jared put it carefully over Tania. He barely heard the van doors close as he drew her into his arms so that she was lying across his lap and cradled against the cushion of his shoulder.

She was very light, yet there was a solid warmth about her that was vaguely comforting. It reminded him of the vitality and strength that usually glowed from her like an aura, and God knew he needed that memory now. His arms tightened about her protectively as the driver started the engine and then drove slowly and cautiously up the road toward the chateau.

It was strange to experience this feeling of belonging to another human being after all those years of standing alone. Strange and a little painful. He wasn't sure he liked it. The emotion had too many sharp edges, and it would probably take time to round them off before he'd feel comfortable with it. Well, he had all the time he needed, and he'd better start adjusting now, because he knew it wasn't going to go away.

He had called it an obsession, and it certainly had been that. She had amused and challenged him at every turn, sparking off him like a small firecracker, arousing him to sexual frenzy one moment and touching off that melting tenderness in him the next. He hadn't really allowed himself to think beyond their time together at the chateau. Perhaps he'd been a little afraid to face the commitment he'd seen glimmering on the horizon the first night he'd met her. Now that commitment wasn't on the horizon, it was here in his arms. The knowledge had exploded within him with the same force as the bullet that had struck her, destroying all the unessentials as if they'd never been.

"Jared."

It was a mere ribbon of a whisper, but he heard it, and his gaze flew down to meet the brilliant darkness of her own. The vitality of her expressive eyes made the fragility and pallor of her face even more apparent, and he felt a thrill of fear course through him. "Are you in any pain?" he asked quickly.

She thought a moment. "A little."

"I've given you a shot. You should be more comfortable very soon."

"I'm comfortable now." She nestled closer to him. "I feel so warm and safe." She shivered. "I was frightened, Jared. I don't think I've ever been as frightened in my life." Her words were becoming slurred as the sedative took effect, and they were spoken with a childlike simplicity. "Hanging there in the darkness knowing—"

"Don't think about it," he said huskily. "It's over and you're safe." His arms tightened about her. "You'll always be safe now."